INVADERS FROM THE INFINITE

MORE WILDSIDE CLASSICS

The Black Star Passes, by John W. Campbell, Jr.
Warlord of Kor, by Terry Carr
Brigands of the Moon, by Ray Cummings
Police Your Planet, by Lester del Rey
The Last Spaceship, by Murray Leinster
The Time Traders, by Andre Norton
Star Surgeon, by Alan E. Nourse
A Planet for Texans, by H. Beam Piper
The White Sybil, by Clark Ashton Smith
An Antarctic Mystery, by Jules Verne

Please see www.wildsidebooks.com for a complete list.

INVADERS FROM THE INFINITE

JOHN W. CAMPBELL, JR.

WILDSIDE PRESS

INVADERS FROM THE INFINITE

This edition published in 2007 by Wildside Press, LLC.
www.wildsidebooks.com

CHAPTER I

INVADERS

Russ Evans, Pilot 3497, Rocket Squad Patrol 34, unsnapped his seat belt, and with a slight push floated "up" into the air inside the weightless ship. He stretched himself, and yawned broadly.

"Red, how soon do we eat?" he called.

"Shut up, you'll wake the others," replied a low voice from the rear of the swift little patrol ship. "See anything?"

"Several million stars," replied Evans in a lower voice. "And —" His tone became suddenly severe. "Assistant Murphy, remember your manners when addressing your superior officer. I've a mind to report you."

A flaming head of hair topping a grinning face poked around the edge of the door. "Lower your wavelength, lower your wavelength! You may think you're a sun, but you're just a planetoid. But what I'd like to know, Chief Pilot Russ Evans, is why they locate a ship in a forlorn, out of the way place like this — three-quarters of a billion miles, out of planetary plane. No ships ever come out here, no pirates, not a chance to help a wrecked ship. All we can do is sit here and watch the other fellows do the work."

"Which is exactly why we're here. Watch — and tell the other ships where to go, and when. Is that chow ready?" asked Russ looking at a small clock giving New York time.

"Uh — think she'll be on time? Come on an' eat."

Evans took one more look at the telectroscope screen, then snapped it off. A tiny, molecular towing unit in his hand, he pointed toward the door to the combined galley and lunch room, and glided in the wake of Murphy.

"How much fuel left?" he asked, as he glided into the dizzily spinning room. A cylindrical room, spinning at high speed, causing an artificial "weight" for the foods and materials in it, made eating of food a less difficult task. Expertly, he maneuvered himself to the guide rail near the center of the room, and caught the spiral. Braking himself into motion, he soon glided down its length, and landed on his feet. He bent and flexed his muscles, waiting for the now-busied assistant to get to the floor and reply.

"They gave us two pounds extra. Lord only knows why. Must expect us to clean up on some fleet. That makes four pound rolls left, untouched, and two thirds of the original pound. We've been here fifteen days, and have six more to go. The main driving power rolls have about the same amount left, and three pound rolls in each reserve bin," replied Red, holding a curiously moving coffee pot that strove to adjust itself to rapidly changing air velocities as it neared the center of the room.

"Sounds like a fleet's power stock. Martian lead or the terrestrial isotope?" asked Evans, tasting warily a peculiar dish before him. "Say, this is energy food. I thought we didn't get any more till Saturday." The change from the energy-less, flavored pastes that made up the principal bulk of a space-pilot's diet, to prevent overeating, when no energy was used in walking in the weightless ship, was indeed a welcome change.

"Uh-huh. I got hungry. Any objections?" grinned the Irishman.

"None!" replied Evans fervently, pitching in with a will.

Seated at the controls once more, he snapped the little switch that caused the screen to glow with flashing, swirling colors as the telectroscope apparatus came to life. A thousand tiny points of flame appeared scattered on a black field with a suddenness that made them seem to snap suddenly into being. Points, tiny dimensionless points of light, save one, a tiny disc of blue-white flame, old Sol from a distance of close to one billion miles, and under slight reverse magnification. The skillful hands at the controls were turning adjustments now, and that disc of flame seemed to leap toward him with a hundred light-speeds, growing to a disc as large as a dime in an instant, while the myriad points of the stars seemed to scatter like frightened chickens, fleeing from the growing sun, out of the screen. Other points, heretofore invisible, appeared, grew, and rushed away.

The sun shifted from the center of the screen, and a smaller reddish-green disc came into view — a planet, its atmosphere coloring the light that left it toward the red. It rushed nearer, grew larger. Earth spread as it took the center of the screen. A world, a portion of a world, a continent, a fragment of a continent as the magnification increased, boundlessly it seemed.

Finally, New York spread across the screen; New York seen from the air, with a strange lack of perspective. The buildings did not seem all to slant toward some point, but to stand vertical, for, from a distance of a billion miles, the vision lines were practically parallel. Titanic shafts of glowing color in the early summer sun appeared; the hot rays from the sun, now only 82,500,000 miles away, shimmering on the colored metal walls.

The new Airlines Building, a mile and a half high, supported at various points by actual spaceship driving units, was a riot of shifting, rainbow hues. A new trick in construction had been used here, and Evans smiled at it. Arcot, inventor of the ship that carried him, had suggested it to Fuller, designer of that ship, and of that building. The colored berylium metal of the wall had been ruled with 20,000 lines to the inch, mere scratches, but nevertheless a diffraction grating. The result was amazingly beautiful. The sunlight, split up to its rainbow colors, was reflected in millions of shifting tints.

In the air, supported by tiny packs strapped to their backs, thousands of people were moving, floating where they wished, in any direction, at any elevation. There were none of the helicopters of even five years ago, now. A molecular power suit was far more convenient, cost nothing to operate, and but $50 to buy. Perfectly safe, requiring no skill, everyone owned them. To the watcher in space, they were mere moving, snaky lines of barely distinguishable dots that shivered and seemed to writhe in the refractions of the air. Passing over them, seeming to pass almost through them in this strange perspectiveless view, were the shadowy forms of giant space liners, titanic streamlined hulls. They were streamlined for no good reason, save that they looked faster and more graceful than the more efficient spherical freighters, just as passenger liners of two centuries earlier, with their steam engines, had carried four funnels and used two. A space liner spent so minute a portion of its journey in the atmosphere that it was really inefficient to streamline them.

"Won't be long!" muttered Russ, grinning cheerily at the familiar, sunlit city. His eyes darted to the chronometer beside him. The view seemed to be taken from a ship that was suddenly scudding across the heavens like a frightened thing, as it ran across from Manhattan Island, followed the Hudson for a short way, then cut across into New Jersey, swinging over the great woodland area of Kittatiny Park, resting finally on the New Jersey suburb of New York nestled in the Kittatinies, Blairtown. Low apartment buildings, ten or twelve stories high, nestled in the waving green of trees in the old roadways. When ground traffic ceased, the streets had been torn up, and parkways substituted.

Quickly the view singled out a single apartment, and the great smooth roof was enlarged on the screen to the absolute maximum clarity, till further magnification simply resulted in worse stratospheric distortion. On the broad roof were white strips of some material, making a huge V followed by two I's. Russ watched, his hand on the control steadying the view under the Earth's complicated orbital motion, and rotation, further corrections for the ship's orbital motion making the job one requiring great skill. The view held the center with amazing clarity. Something seemed to be happening to the last of the I's. It crumpled suddenly, rolled in on itself and disappeared.

"She's there, and on time," grinned Russ happily.

He tried more magnification. Could he —

He was tired, terribly, suddenly tired. He took his hands from the viewplate controls, relaxed, and dropped off to sleep.

"What made me so tired — wonder — GOD!" He straightened with a jerk, and his hands flew to the controls. The view on the machine suddenly retreated, flew back with a velocity inconceivable. Earth dropped away from the ship with an apparent velocity a thousand times that of light; it was a tiny ball, a pinpoint, gone, the sun — a minute disc — gone — then the apparatus was flashing views into focus from the other side of the ship. The assistant did not reply. Evans' hands were growing ineffably heavy, his whole body yearned for sleep. Slowly, clumsily he pawed for a little stud. Somehow his hand found it, and the ship reeled suddenly, little jerks, as the code message was flung out in a beam of such tremendous power that the sheer radiation pressure made it noticeable. Earth would be notified. The system would be warned. But light, slow crawling thing, would take hours to cross the gulf of space, and radio travels no faster.

Half conscious, fighting for his faculties with all his will, the pilot turned to the screen. A ship! A strange, glistening thing streamlined to the nth degree, every spare corner rounded till the resistance was at the irreducible minimum. But, in the great pilotport of the stranger, the patrol pilot saw faces, and gasped in surprise as he saw them! Terrible faces, blotched, contorted. Patches of white skin, patches of brown, patches of black, blotched and twisted across the faces. Long, lean faces, great wide flat foreheads above, skulls strangely squared, more box-like than man's rounded skull. The ears were large, pointed tips at the top. Their hair was a silky mane that extended low over the forehead, and ran back, spreading above the ears, and down the neck.

Then, as that emotion of surprise and astonishment weakened his will momentarily, oblivion came, with what seemed a fleeting instant of memories. His life seemed to flash before his mind in serried rank, a file of events, his childhood, his life, his marriage, his wife, an image of smiling comfort, then the years, images of great and near great men, his knowledge of history, pictures of great war of 2074, pictures of the attackers of the Black Star — then calm oblivion, quiet blankness.

The long, silent ship that had hovered near him turned, and pointed toward the pinhead of matter that glowed brilliantly in the flaming jewel box of the heavens. It was gone in an instant, rushing toward Sun and Earth at a speed that outraced the flying radio message, leaving the ship of the Guard Patrol behind, and leaving the Pilot as he leaves our story.

CHAPTER II

CANINE PEOPLE

"And that," said Arcot between puffs, "will certainly be a great boon to the Rocket Patrol, you must admit. They don't like dueling with these space-pirates using the molecular rays, and since molecular rays have such a tremendous commercial value, we can't prohibit the sale of ray apparatus. Now, if you will come into the 'workshop,' Fuller, I'll give a demonstration with friend Morey's help."

The four friends rose, Morey, Wade and Fuller following Arcot into his laboratory on the thirty-seventh floor of the Arcot Research Building. As they went, Arcot explained to Fuller the results and principles of the latest product of the ingenuity of the "Triumvirate," as Arcot, Morey and Wade had come to be called in the news dispatches.

"As you know, the molecular rays make all the molecules of any piece of matter they are turned upon move in the desired direction. Since they supply no new energy, but make the body they are turned upon supply its own, using the energy of its own random molecular motion of heat, they are practically impossible to stop. The energy necessary for molecular rays to take effect is so small that the usual type of filter lets enough of it pass. A ship equipped with filters is no better off when attacked than one without. The rays simply drove the front end into the rear, or *vice versa*, or tore it to pieces as the pirates desired. The Rocket Patrol could kill off the pirates, but they lost so many men in the process, it was a Phyrric victory.

"For some time Morey and I have been working on something to stop the rays. Obviously it can't be by means of any of the usual metallic energy absorption screens.

"We finally found a combination of rays, better frequencies, that did what we wanted. I have such an apparatus here. What we want you to do, of course, is the usual job of rearranging the stuff so that the apparatus can be made from dies, and put into quantity production. As the Official Designer for the A.A.L. you ought to do that easily." Arcot grinned as Fuller looked in amazement at the apparatus Arcot had picked up from the bench in the "workshop."

"Don't get worried," laughed Morey, "that's got a lifting unit combined — just a plain ordinary molecular lift such as you see by the hundreds out there." Morey pointed through the great window where thousands of those lift units were carrying men, women and children through the air, lifting them hundreds, thousands of feet above the streets and through the doors of buildings.

"Here's an ordinary molecular pistol. I'm going to put the suit on, and rise about five feet off the floor. You can turn the pistol on me, and see what impression it makes on the suit."

Fuller took the molecular ray pistol, while Wade helped Arcot into the suit. He looked at the pistol dubiously, pointed it at a heavy casting of iron resting in one corner of the room, and turned the ray at low concentration, then pressed the trigger-button. The casting gave out a low, scrunching grind, and slid toward him with a lurch. Instantly he shut off the power. "This isn't any ordinary pistol. It's got seven or eight times the ordinary power!" he exclaimed.

"Oh yes, I forgot," Morey said. "Instead of the fuel battery that the early pistols used, this has a space-distortion power coil. This pistol has as much power as the usual A-39 power unit for commercial work."

By the time Morey had explained the changes to Fuller, Arcot had the suit on, and was floating five or six feet in the air, like a grotesque captive balloon. "Ready, Fuller?"

"I guess so, but I certainly hope that suit is all it is claimed to be. If it isn't — well I'd rather not commit murder."

"It'll work," said Arcot. "I'll bet my neck on that!" Suddenly he was surrounded by the faintest of auras, a strange, wavering blue light, like the hazy corona about a 400,000-volt power line. "Now try it."

Fuller pointed the pistol at the floating man and pushed the trigger. The brilliant blue beam of the molecular ray, and the low hum of the air, rushing in the path of the director beam, stabbed out toward Arcot. The faint aura about him was suddenly intensified a million times till he floated in a ball of blue-white fire. Scarcely visible, the air about him blazed with bluish incandescence of ionization.

"Increase the power," suggested Morey. Fuller turned on more power. The blue halo was shot through with tiny violet sparks, the sharp odor of ozone in the air was stifling; the heat of wasted energy was making the room hotter. The power increased further, and the tiny sparks were waving streamers, that laced across the surface of the blue fire. Little jets of electric flame reached out along the beam of the ray now. Finally, as full power of the molecular ray was reached, the entire halo was buried under a mass of writhing sparks that seemed to leap up into the air above the man's head, wavering up to extinction. The room was unbearably hot, despite the molecular ray coolers absorbing the heat of the air, and blowing cooled air into the room.

Fuller snapped off the ray, and put the pistol on the table beside him. The halo died, and went out a moment later, and Arcot settled to the floor.

"This particular suit will stand up against anything the ordinary commercial sets will give. The system now: remember that the rays are short electrical waves. The easiest way to stop them is to interpose a wave of opposite phase, and cause interference. Fine, but try to get in tune with an unknown wave when it is moving in relation to your center of control. It is impossible to do it before you yourself have been rayed out of existence. We must use some system that will automatically, instantly be out of phase.

"The Hall effect would naturally tend to make the frequency of a wave through a resisting medium change, and lengthen. If we can send out a spherical wave front, and have it lengthen rapidly as it proceeds, we will have a wave front that is, at all points, different. Any entering wave would, sooner or later, meet a wave that was half a phase out, no matter what the motion was, nor what the frequency, as long as it lies within the comparatively narrow molecular wave band. What this apparatus, or ray screen, consists of, is a machine generating a spherical wave front of the nature of a molecular wave, but of just too great a frequency to do anything. A second part generates a condition in space, which opposes that wave. After traveling a certain distance, the wave has lengthened to molecular wave type, but is now beyond the machine which generated it, and no longer affects it, or damages it. However, as it proceeds, it continues to lengthen, till eventually it reaches the length of infra-light, when the air quickly absorbs it, as it reaches one of the absorption bands for air molecular waves, and any molecular wave must find its half-wave complement somewhere in that wedge of waves. It does, and is at once choked off, its energy fighting the energy of the ray screen, of course. In the air, however, the screen is greatly helped by the fact that before the half-wave frequency is met in the ray-wedge, the molecular ray is buried in ions, leaving the ray screen little work to do.

"Now your job is to design the apparatus in a form that machines can make automatically. We tried doing it ourselves for the fun of it, but we couldn't see how we could make a machine that didn't need at least two humans to supervise."

"Well," grinned Fuller, "you have it all over me as scientists, but as economic workers — two human supervisors to make one product!"

"All right — we agree. But no, let's see you — Lord! What was that?" Morey started for the door on the run. The building was still trembling from the shock of a heavy blow, a blow that seemed much as though a machine had been wrecked on the armored roof, and a big machine at that. Arcot, a flying suit already on, was up in the air, and darting past Morey in an instant, streaking for the vertical shaft that would let him out to the roof. The molecular ray pistol was already in his hand, ready to pull any beams off unfortunate victims pinned under them.

In a moment he had flashed up through the seven stories, and out to the roof. A gigantic silvery machine rested there, streamlined to perfection, its hull dazzlingly beautiful in the sunlight. A door opened, and three tall, lean men stepped from it. Already people were collecting about the ship, flying up from below. Air patrolmen floated up in a minute, and seeing Arcot, held the crowd back.

The strange men were tall, eight feet or more in height. Great, round, soft brown eyes looked in curiosity at the towering multi-colored buildings, at the people floating in the air, at the green trees and the blue sky, the yellowish sun.

Arcot looked at their strangely blotched and mottled heads, faces, arms and hands. Their feet were very long and narrow, their legs long and thin. Their faces were kindly; the mottled skin, brown and white and black, seemed not to make them ugly. It was not a disfigurement; it seemed oddly familiar and natural in some reminiscent way.

"Lord, Arcot — queer specimens, yet they seem familiar!" said Morey in an undertone.

"They are. Their race is that of man's first and best friend, the dog! See the brown eyes? The typical teeth? The feet still show the traces of the dog's toe-step. Their nails, not flat like human ones but rounded? The mottled skin, the ears — look, one is advancing."

One of the strangers walked laboriously forward. A lighter world than Earth was evidently his home. His great brown eyes fixed themselves on Arcot's. Arcot watched them. They seemed to expand, grow larger; they seemed to fill all the sky. Hypnotism! He concentrated his mind, and the eyes suddenly contracted to the normal eyes of the stranger. The man reeled back, as Arcot's telepathic command to sleep came, stronger than his own will. The stranger's friends caught him, shook him, but he slept. One of the others looked at Arcot; his eyes seemed hurt, desperately pleading.

Arcot strode forward, and quickly brought the man out of the trance. He shook his head, smiled at Arcot, then, with desperate difficulty, he enunciated some words in English, terribly distorted.

"Ahy wizz tahk. Vokle kohds ron. Tahk by breen."

Distorted as it was, Arcot recognized the meaning without difficulty. "I wish (to) talk. Vocal cords wrong. Talk by brain." He switched to communication by the Venerian method, telepathically, but without hypnotism.

"Good enough. When you attempted to hypnotize me, I didn't known what you wanted. It is not necessary to hypnotize to carry on communication by the method of the second world of this system. What brings you to our system? From what system do you come? What do you wish to say?"

The other, not having learned the Venerian system, had great difficulty in communicating his thoughts, but Arcot learned that they had machines which would make it easier, and the terrestrian invited them into his laboratory, for the crowd was steadily growing.

The three returned to their ship for a moment, coming out with several peculiar headsets. Almost at once the ship started to rise, going up more and more swiftly, as the people cleared a way for it.

Then, in the tiniest fraction of a second, the ship was gone; it shrank to a point, and was invisible in the blue vault of the sky.

"Apparently they intend to stay a while," said Wade. "They are trusting souls, for their line of retreat is cut off. We naturally have no intention of harming them, but they can't know that."

"I'm not so sure," said Arcot. He turned to the apparent leader of the three and explained that there were several stories to descend, and stairs were harder than a flying unit. "Wrap your arms about my legs, when I rise above you, and hold on till your feet are on the floor again," he concluded.

The stranger walked a little closer to the edge of the shaft, and looked down. White bulbs illuminated its walls down its length to the ground. The man talked rapidly to his friends, looking with evident distaste at the shaft, and the tiny pack on Arcot's back. Finally, smiling, he evinced his willingness. Arcot rose, the man grasped his legs, and then both rose. Over the shaft, and down to his laboratory was the work of a moment.

Arcot led them into his "consultation room," where a number of comfortable chairs were arranged, facing each other. He seated them together, and his own friends facing them.

"Friends of another world," began Arcot, "we do not know your errand here, but you evidently have good reason for coming to this place. It is unlikely that your landing was the result of sheer chance. What brought you? How came you to this point?"

"It is difficult for me to reply. First we must be *en rapport*. Our system is not simple as yours, but more effective, for yours depends on thought ideas, not altogether universal. Place these on your heads, for only a moment. I must induce temporary hypnotic coma. Let one try first if you desire." The leader of the visitors held out one of the several headsets they had brought, caplike things, made of laminated metal apparently.

Arcot hesitated, then with a grin slipped it on.

"Relax," came a voice in Arcot's head, a low, droning voice, a voice of command. "Sleep," it added. Arcot felt himself floating down an infinite shaft, on some superflying suit that did not pull at him with its straps, just floating down lightly, down and down and down. Suddenly he reached the bottom, and found to his surprise that it led directly into the room again! He was back. "You are awake. Speak!" came the voice.

Arcot shook himself, and looked about. A new voice spoke now, not the tonelessly melodious voice, but the voice of an individual, yet a mental voice. It was perfectly clear, and perfectly comprehensible. "We have traveled far to find you, and now we have business of the utmost import. Ask these others to let us treat them, for we must do what we can in the least possible time. I will explain when all can understand. I am Zezdon Fentes, First Student of Thought. He who sits on my right is Zezdon Afthen, and he beyond him, is Zezdon Inthel, of Physics and of Chemistry, respectively."

And now Arcot spoke to his friends.

"These men have something of the greatest importance to tell us, it seems. They want us all to hear, and they are in a hurry. The treatment isn't at all annoying. Try it. The man on the extreme right, as we face them, is Zezdon Fentes of Thought, Zezdon apparently meaning something like professor, or 'First Student of.' Those next him are Zezdon Afthen of Physics and Zezdon Inthel of Chemistry."

Zezdon Afthen offered them the headsets, and in a moment everyone present was wearing one. The process of putting them *en rapport* took very little time, and shortly all were able to communicate with ease.

"Friends of Earth, we must tell our strange story quickly for the benefit of your world as well as ours, and others, too. We cannot so much as annoy. We are helpless to combat them.

"Our world lies far out across the galaxy; even with incalculable velocity of the great swift thing that bore us, three long months have we traveled toward your distant worlds, hoping that at last the Invaders might meet their masters.

"We landed on this roof because we examined mentally the knowledge of a pilot of one of your patrol ships. His mind told us that here we would find the three greatest students of Science of this Solar System. So it was here we came for help.

"Our race has arisen," he continued, "as you have so surely determined from the race you call canines. It was artificially produced by the Ancient Masters when their hour of need had come. We have lost the great science of the Ancient Ones. But we have developed a different science, a science of the mind."

"Dogs are far more psychic than are men. They would naturally tend to develop such a civilization," said Arcot judiciously.

CHAPTER III

A QUARTER OF A MILLION LIGHT YEARS

"Our civilization," continued Zezdon Afthen, "is built largely on the knowledge of the mind. We cannot have criminals, for the man who plots evil is surely found out by his thoughts. We cannot have lying politicians and unjust rulers.

"It is a peaceful civilization. The Ancient Masters feared and hated War with a mighty aversion. But they did not make our race cowards, merely peaceful intelligence. Now we must fight for our homes, and my race will fight mightily. But we need weapons.

"But my story has little to do with our race. I will tell the story of our civilization and of the Ancient Ones later when the time is more auspicious.

"Four months ago, our mental vibration instruments detected powerful emanations from space. That could only mean that a new, highly intelligent race had suddenly appeared within a billion miles of our world. The directional devices quickly spotted it as emanating from the third planet of our system. Zezdon Fentes, with my aid, set up some special apparatus, which would pick up strong thoughts and make them visible. We had used this before to see not only what an enemy looked upon, but also what he saw in that curious thing, the eye of the mind, the vision of the past and the future. But while the thought-amplification device was powerful, the new emanations were hard to separate from each other.

"It was done finally, when all but one man slept. That one we were enable to tune sharply to. After that we could reach him at any time. He was the commander. We saw him operate the ship, we saw the ship, saw it glide over the barren, rocky surface of that world. We saw other men come in and go out. They were strange men. Short, squat, bulky men. Their arms were short and stocky. But their strength was enormous, unbelievable. We saw them bend solid bars of steel as thick as my arm. With perfect ease!

"Their brains were tremendously active, but they were evil, selfishly evil. Nothing that did not benefit them counted. At one time our instruments went dead, and we feared that the commander had detected us, but we saw what happened a little later. The second in command had killed him.

"We saw them examine the world, working their way across it, wearing heavy suits, yet, for all the terrific gravity of that world, bouncing about like rubber balls, leaping and jumping where they wanted. Their legs would drive out like pistons, and they soared up and through the air.

"They were tired while they made those examinations, and slept heavily at night.

"Then one night there was a conference. We saw then what they intended. Before we had tried desperately to signal them. Now we were glad that we had failed.

"We saw their ship rise (in the thoughts of the second in command) and sail out into space, and rush toward our world. The world grew larger, but it was imperfectly sketched in, for they did not know our world well. Their telescopes did not have great power as your electric telescopes have.

"We saw them investigate the planet. We saw them plan to destroy any people they found with a ray which was as follows: 'the ray which makes all parts move as one.' We could not understand and could not interpret. Thoughts beyond our knowledge have, of course, no meaning, even when our mental amplifiers get them, and bring them to us."

"The Molecular ray!" gasped Morey in surprise. "They will be an enemy."

"You know it! It is familiar to you! You have it? You can fight it?" asked Zezdon Afthen excitedly.

"We know it, and can fight it, if that is all they have."

"They have more — much more I fear," replied Zezdon Afthen. "At any rate, we saw what they intended. If our world was inhabited, they would destroy every one on it, and then other men of their race were to float in on their great ships, and settle on that largest of our worlds.

"We had to stop them so we did what we could. We had powerful machines, which would amplify and broadcast our thoughts. So we broadcast our thought-waves, and implanted in the mind of their leader that it would be wise to land, and learn the extent of the civilization, and the weapons to be met. Also, as the ship drew nearer, we made him decide on a certain spot we had prepared for him.

"He never guessed that the thoughts were not his own. Only the ideas came to him, seeming to spring from his own mind.

"He landed — and we used our one weapon. It was a thing left to one group of rulers when the Ancient Masters left us to care for ourselves. What it was, we never knew; we had never used it in the fifteen thousand years since the Great Masters had passed — never had to. But now it was brought out, and concealed behind great piles of rock in a deep canyon where the ship of the enemy would land. When it landed, we turned the beam of the machine on it, and the apparatus rotated it swiftly, and a cone of the beam's ray was formed as the beam was swung through a small circle in the vertical plane. The machine leaped backward, and though it was so massive that a tremendous amount of labor had been required to bring it there, the push of the pencil of force we sent out hurled it back against a rocky cliff behind it as though it were some child's toy. It continued to operate for perhaps a second, perhaps two. In that time two great holes had been cut in the enemy ship, holes fifteen feet across, that ran completely through the hull as though a die had cut through the metal of the ship, cutting out a disc of metal.

"There was a terrific concussion, and a roar as the air blasted out of the ship. It did not take us long to discover that the enemy were dead. Their terrible, bloated corpses lay everywhere in the ship. Most of the men we were able to recognize, having seen them in the mentovisor. But the colors were distorted, and their forms were peculiar. Indeed, the whole ship seemed strange. The only time that things ever did seem normal about that strange thing, when the angles of it seemed what they were, when the machines did not seem out of proportion, out of shape, twisted, was when on a trial trip we ventured very close to our sun."

Arcot whistled softly and looked at Morey. Morey nodded. "Probably right. Don't interrupt."

"That you thought something, I understood, but the thoughts themselves were hopelessly unintelligible to me. You know the explanation?" asked Zezdon Afthen eagerly.

"We think so. The ship was evidently made on a world of huge size. Those men, their stocky, block legs and arms, their entire build and their desire for the largest of your planets, would indicate that. Their own world was probably even larger — they were forced to wear pressure suits even on that large world, and could jump all over, you said. On so huge a sphere as their native world seems to be, the gravity would be so intense as to distort space. Geometry, such as yours seems to be, and such as ours was, could never be developed, for you assume the existence of a straight line, and of an absolute plane surface. These things cannot exist in space, but on small worlds, far from the central sun's mass, the conditions approach that without sufficient discrepency to make the error obvious. On so huge a globe as their world the space is so curved that it is at once obvious that no straight line exists, and that no plane exists. Their geometry would never be like ours. When you went close to your sun, the attraction was sufficient to curve space into a semblance of the natural conditions on their home planet, then your senses and the ship met a compromise condition which made it seem more or less normal, not so obviously strange to you.

"But continue." Arcot looked at Afthen interestedly.

"There were none left in their ship now, and we had been careful in locating the first hole, that it should not damage the propulsive machinery. The second hole was accidental, due to the shift of the machine. The machine itself was wrecked now, crushed by its own reaction. We forgot that any pencil of force powerful enough to do what we wanted, would tear the machine from its moorings unless fastened with great steel bolts into the solid rock.

"The second hole had been far to the rear, and had, by ill-luck, cut out a portion of the driving apparatus. We could not repair that, though we did succeed at last in lifting the great discs into place. We attempted to cut them, and put them back in sections. Our finest saws and machines did not nick them. Their weight was unbelievable, and yet we finally succeeded in lifting the things into the wall of the ship. The actual missing material did not represent more than a tiny cut, perhaps as wide as one of your credit-discs. You could slip the thin piece of metal in between them, but not so much as your finger.

"Those slots we welded tight with our best steel, letting a flap hang over on each side of the cut, and as the hot metal cooled, it was drawn against the shining walls with terrific force. The joints were perfectly airtight.

"The machines proper were repaired to the greatest possible extent. It was a heartbreaking task, for we must only guess at what machines should be connected together. Much damage had been done by the rushing air as it left, for it filled the machines, too, and they were not designed to resist the terrific air pressure that was on them when the pressure in the ship escaped. Many of the machines had been burst open, and these we could repair when we had the necessary elements and knew their construction from the remnants, or could find unbroken duplicates in the stock rooms.

"Once we connected the wrong things. This will show you what we dealt with. They were the wrong poles — two generators, connected together in the wrong way. There was a terrific crash when the switch was thrown, and huge sheets of electric flame leaped from one of them. Two men were killed, incinerated in an instant, even the odors one might expect were killed in that flash of heat. Everything save the shining metal and clear glass within ten feet of it was instantly wiped out. And there was a fuse link that gave. The generator was ruined. One was left, and several small auxiliary generators.

"Eventually, we did the job. We made the machine work. And we are here.

"We have come to warn you, and to ask aid. Your system also has a large planet, slightly smaller than the largest of our system, but yet attractive. There are approximately 50,000 planetary systems in this universe, according to the records of the Invaders. Their world is not of this system. It is the World Thett, sun Antseck, Universe Venone. Where that is, or even what it means, we do not know. Perhaps you understand.

"But they investigated your world, and its address, according to their records, was World 3769-8482730-3. This, I believe, means, Universe 3769, sun 8482730, world 3. They have been investigating this system now for nearly three centuries. It was close to 200 years ago that they visited your world — two hundred years of your time."

"This is 2129 — which makes it about the year 1929-30 that they floated around here investigating. Why haven't they done anything?" Arcot asked him.

"They waited for an auspicious time. They are afraid now, for recently they visited your world, and were utterly amazed to find the unbelievable progress your people have made. They intend to make an immediate attack on all worlds known to be intelligently populated. They had made the mistake of letting one race learn too much; they cannot afford to let it happen again.

"There are only twenty-one inhabited worlds known, and their thousands of scouts have already investigated nearly all the central mass of this universe, and much of the outer rings. They have established a base in this universe. Where I do not know. That, alone, was never mentioned in the records. But of all peoples, they feared only your world.

"There is one race in the universe far older than yours, but they are a sleeping people. Long ago their culture decayed. Still, now they are not far from you, and perhaps it will be worth the few days needed to learn more about them. We have their location and can take you there. Their world circles a dead star —"

"Not any more," laughed Morey grimly. "That's another surprise for the enemy. They had a little jog, and they certainly are wide awake now. They are headed for big things, and they are going to do a lot."

"But how do you know these things? You have ships that can go from planet to planet, I know, but the records of the enemy said you could not leave the system of your sun. They alone knew that secret."

"Another surprise for them," said Morey. "We can — and we can move faster than your ship, if not faster than they. The people of the dead star have moved to a very live star — Sirius, the brightest in our heavens. And they are as much alive now as their new sun. They can move faster than light, also. We had a little misunderstanding a while back, when their star passed close to ours. They came off second best, and we haven't spoken to them since. But I think we can make valuable allies there."

For all Morey's jocular manner, he realized the terrible import of this announcement. A race which had been able to cross the vast gulf of intergalactic space in the days when Terrestrians were still developing the airplane — and already they had mapped Jupiter, and planned their colonies! What developments had come? They had molecular rays, cosmic rays, the energy of matter, then — what else had they now? Lux and Relux, the two artificial metals, made of solidified light, far stronger than anything of molecular structure in nature, absolutely infusible, totally inert chemically, one a perfect conductor of light and of all radiation in space, the other a perfect reflector of all radiations — save molecular rays. Made into the condition of reflection by the action of special frequencies in its formation from light, molecular frequencies were, unfortunately, able to convert it into perfectly transparent lux metal, when the protective value was gone.

They had that. All Earth had, perhaps.

"There was one other race of some importance, the others were semi-civilized. They rated us in a position between these races and the high races — yours, those of the dead star, and those of world 3769-37:478:326:894-6. Our science had been investigated two hundred or so years ago.

"This other race was at a great distance from us, greater than yours, and apparently not feared as greatly as yours. They cannot cross to other worlds, save in small ships driven solely by fire, which the Thessians have called a 'hopelessly inefficient and laughably awkward thing to ride in.'"

"Rockets," grinned Morey. "Our first ship was part rocket."

Zezdon Fentes smiled. "But that is all. We have brought you warning, and our plea. Can you help us?"

"We cannot answer that. The Interplanetary Council must act. But I am afraid that it will be all we can do to protect our own world if this enemy attacks soon, and I fear they will. Since they have a base in this universe, it is impossible to believe that all ships did not report back to the home world at stated intervals. That one is missing will soon be discovered, and it will be sought. War will start at once. Three months it took you to reach us — they should come soon.

"Those men who left will be on their way back from the home world from which they came. What do you call your planet, friend?"

"Ortol is our home," replied Zezdon Inthel.

"At any rate, I can only assure you that your world will be given weapons that will permit your people to defend themselves and I will get you to your home within twenty-four hours. Your ship — is it in the system?"

"It waits on the second satellite of the fourth planet," replied Zezdon Afthen.

"Signal them, and tell them to land where a beacon of intense light, alternating red and blue, reaches up from — this point on the map." Arcot pointed out the spot in Vermont where their private lake and laboratory were.

He turned to the others, and in rapid-fire English, explained his plans. "We need the help of these people as much as they need ours. I think Zezdon Fentes will stay here and help you. The others will go with us to their world. There we shall have plenty of work to do, but on the way we are going to stop at Mars and pick up that valuable ship of theirs and make a careful examination for possible new weapons, their system of speed-drive, and their regular space-drive. I'm willing to make a bet right now, that I can guess both. Their regular drive is a molecular drive with lead disintegration apparatus for the energy, cosmic ray absorbers for the heating, and a drive much like ours. Their speed drive is a time distortion apparatus, I'll wager. Time distinction offers an easy solution of speed. All speed is relative — relative to other bodies, but also to time-speed. But we'll see.

"I'm going to hustle some workmen to installing the biggest spare power board I can get into the storerooms of the *Ancient Mariner*, and pack in a ray-screen. It will be useful. Let's move."

"Our ship," said Zezdon Afthen, "will land in three of your hours."

CHAPTER IV

THE FIRST MOVE

The Ortolians were standing on a low, green-clad hill. Below them stretched the green flank of the little rise, and beyond lay ridge after ridge of the broad, smooth carpet of the beautiful Vermont hills.

"Man of Earth," said Zezdon Afthen, turning at last to Wade, who stood behind him. "It took us three months of constant flight at a speed unthinkable, through space dotted with the titanic gems of the Outer Dark, stars gleaming in red, and blue and orange, some titanic lighthouses of our course, others dim pinpoints of glowing color. It was a scene of unspeakable grandeur, but it was so awesomely mighty in its scope, one was afraid, and his soul shriveled within him as he looked at those inconceivable masses floating forever alone in the silence of the inconceivable nothingness of eternal cold and eternal darkness. One was awed, suppressed by their sheer magnitude. A magnificent spectacle truly, but one no man could love.

"Now we are at rest on a tiny pinpoint of dust in a tiny bit of a tiny corner of an isolated universe, and the magnitude and stillness is gone. Only the chirpings of those strange birds as they seek rest in darkness, the soft gurgling of the little stream below, and the rustle of countless leaves, break the silence with a satisfying existence, while the loneliness of that great star, your sun, is lost in its tintings of soft color, the fleeciness of the clouds, and the seeming companionship of green hills.

"The beauty of boundless space is awe-inspiring in its magnitude. The beauty of Earth is something man can love.

"Man of Earth, you have a home that you may well fight for with all the strength of your arms, all the forces of your brain, and all the energies of Space that you can call forth to aid you. It is a wondrous world." Silently he stood in the gathering dusk, as first Venus winked into being, then one by one the stars came into existence in the deepening color of the sky.

"Space is awesomely wonderful; this is — lovable." He gazed long at the heavens of this world so strange, so beautiful to him, looking at the unfamiliar heavens, as star after star flashed into the constellations so familiar to terrestrials and to those Venerians who had been above the clouds of Venus' eternal shroud.

"But somewhere off there in space are other races, and far

beyond the power of our eyes to see is the star that is the sun of my world, and around it circles that little globe that is home to me. What is happening there now? Does it still exist? Are there people still living on it? Oh, Man of Earth, let us reach that world quickly, you cannot guess the pangs that attack me, for if it be destroyed, think — forever I am without home — without friends I knew. However kind your people may be to me, I would be forever lonely.

"I will not think of that — only it is time your ship was ready, is it not?"

"I think we had better return," replied Wade softly, his English words rousing thoughts in his mind intelligible to the Ortolians.

The three rose in the air on the molecular suits and drove quickly down toward the blue gem of the lake to the east, nestled among still other green hills. Lights were showing in the great shop, where the *Ancient Mariner* was being fitted with the ray-shields, and all possible weapons. Men streaming through her were hastily stocking her with vast quantities of foods, stocks of fuel, all the spare parts they could cram into her stock rooms.

When the men arrived from the hilltop, the work was practically done, and Wade stepped up to Morey, busily checking off a list of required items.

"Everything you ordered came through?" he asked.

"Yes — thanks to the pull of a two-billion dollar private fortune. Who says credit-units don't have their value? This expedition never would have gotten through, if it hadn't been for that.

"But we have the main space distortion power bank, and the new auxiliary coils full. Ten tons of lead aboard for fuel. There's one thing we are afraid of. If the enemy have a system of tubes that is able to handle more power than our last tube — we're sunk. These brilliant people that suggest using more tubes to a ray-power bank forget the last tube has to handle the entire output of all the others, and modulate it correctly. If the enemy has a better tube — it will be too bad for us." Morey was frankly worried.

"My end is all set, Morey. How soon will you be ready?" Arcot asked.

"'Bout ten-fifteen minutes." Morey lit a cigarette and watched as the last of the stuff was carried aboard.

At last they were ready. The *Ancient Mariner*, originally built for intergalactic exploration, was kept in working condition. New apparatus had been incorporated in it, as their research had led to improvements, and it was constantly in condition, ready for a trip. Many exploration trips to the nearer stars had already been made.

The ship was backed out from the hangar now, and rested on the great smooth landing field, its tremendous quarter million ton mass of lux and relux sinking a great, smooth depression in the turf of the field. They were waiting now for the arrival of the Ortolian ship. Zezdon Afthen assured them it would be there in a few minutes.

High in the sky, came the whining whistle of an approaching ship, coming at terrific velocity. It came nearer the field, darting toward the ground at an unheard of speed, flashing down at a speed of well over three thousand miles an hour, and, only in the last fifty feet slowed with a sickening deceleration. Even so it landed with a crash of fully two hundred miles of speed. Arcot gasped at the terrible landing the pilot had made, fully expecting to see the great hull dent somewhat, even though made of solid relux. And certainly the jar would kill every man on board. Yet the hull did not seem harmed by the crash, and even the ground under the ship was but slightly disturbed, though, at a distance of some thirty feet, the entire block of soil was crushed, and cracked by the terrific impact of hundreds of thousands of tons striking with terrific energy.

"Lord, it's a wonder they didn't kill themselves. I never saw such a rotten landing," exclaimed Morey with disgust.

"Don't be too sure. I think they landed gently, and at very low speed. Notice how little the soil directly under them was dented?" replied Arcot, walking forward. "They have time control, as I suspected. Ask them. They drifted in gently. Their time rate was speeded up tremendously, so that what was hundreds of miles per hour to us was feet per minute to them. But come on, get the handlers to bring that junk up to the door — they are coming out."

One of the tall, kindly-faced canine people was standing in the doorway now, the white light streaming out around him into the night, casting a grotesque shadow on the landing field, for all the flood lights bathing in it.

Zezdon Afthen came up and spoke quickly to the man evidently in command of the ship. The entire party went into the ship, and the cream of their laboratory instruments was brought in.

For hours Arcot, Morey and Wade worked at the apparatus in the ship, measuring, calculating, following electrical and magnetic and sheer force hook-ups of staggering complexity. They were not trying to find the exact method of construction, only the principles involved, so that they could perform calculations of their own, and duplicate the results of the enemy. Thus they would be far more thoroughly familiar with the machinery when done.

Little attention was paid to the actual driving plant, for it was a molecular drive with the same type of lead-fuel burner they used in their own ship. The tubes of the power bank were, however, a puzzle to them. They were made of relux, so that it was impossible to see the interior of the tube. To open one was to destroy it, but calculations made from readings of their instruments showed that they were more efficient, and could readily carry nearly half again the load that the best terrestrian tubes could sustain. This meant the enemy could send heavier rays and heavier ray screens.

But finally they returned to the *Ancient Mariner*, and as the Ortolian ship whined its way out to space, the *Ancient Mariner* started, rising faster and faster through the atmosphere till it was in the night of space. Then the molecular power was shut off. The ship suddenly seemed to writhe, space was black and starless about them, then sparkling weirdly distorted stars, all before them. They were moving already. Almost before the Ortolians fully realized what was happening, a dozen stars had swung past the ship, driving on now at better than five light years in every second. At this speed, approximately fourteen hours would be needed to reach Ortol.

"Now, Arcot, perhaps you will explain to me the secret of this ship," said Zezdon Afthen at last, turning from the great lux pilot's window, to Arcot seated in the pilot's chair. "I know that only the broadest principles will be intelligible to me, for I could not understand that ship we captured, after almost four months of study. Yet it crept through space compared with this ship. Certainly no ship could outdistance this in a race!"

"As a matter of fact — watch!" Arcot pushed a little metal button along a slide to the extreme end. Again the ship seemed to writhe. Space was no longer black, but faintly gray, and beside them, on either side, floated two exact replicas of their ship! Zezdon Afthen stared. But in another moment, both were gone, and space was black, yet in but a few moments a grayness was showing, and light was appearing from all about, growing gradually in intensity. For three seconds Arcot continued thus, then he pulled the metal button down the slide, and flicked over another that he had pulled to cause the second change. The stars were again before them, their colors changed beyond all recognition at that speed. But the orientation of the stars behind them had been familiar. Now an entirely different set of constellation showed.

"I merely opened the ship out to her maximum speed for a

moment. I was able to see any large star 2000 light years in our path, and there were none. Small stars do not bother us as I will explain. When I put on full power of the main power coils, I drove the ship up to a speed of 30 light years a second. When I turned in the full power of the auxiliary coils as well I doubled the power, and the speed was multiplied by eight. The result was that in the four seconds of racing, we made approximately 1000 light years!"

Zezdon Afthen gasped. "Two hundred and forty light years *per second*"! He paused in bewilderment. "Suppose we had struck a small sun, a dark star, even a meteor at that speed? What would have been the result?"

Arcot smiled. "The chances are excellent that we plowed through more than one meteor, more than one dark star, and more than one small sun.

"But this is the secret: the ship attains the speed only by going out of space. *Nothing in space can attain the speed of light, save radiation.* Nothing in normal space. But, we alter space, make space along patterns we choose, and so distort it that the natural speed of radiation is enormously greater. In fact, we so change space that nothing can go *slower* than a speed we fix.

"Morey — show Afthen the coils, and explain it all to him. I've got to stay here."

Morey rose, and diving through the weightless ship, went down to the power room, Zezdon Afthen following. Here, giant pots five feet high were in close packed rows. The "pots" contained specially designed coils storing tremendous energy, the energy of four tons of disintegrated lead, in the only form that energy may be stored, as a strain, or distortion in space. These charged coils distorted only the space within themselves, making a closed field entirely within themselves. But in the exact gravitational center of the quarter of a million ton ship was a single high coil of different design that distorted space around it as well as the space within it. This, as Morey explained, was the control that altered the constants of space to suit. The coils were charged, and the energy stored. Their energy could be pumped into the big coil, and then, when the ship slowed to normal space, could be pumped back to them. The pumping energy, as well as any further energy needed for recharging the coils could be supplied by three huge power generators.

"These energy-producers," Morey explained, "work on a principle known for hundreds of years on Earth. Lead, when reduced to a temperature approaching absolute zero as closely as, for instance, liquid helium, has *no* electrical resistance. In other words, no matter how great a current is sent through it, there is no resistance, and no heat is produced to raise the temperature. What we do is to send a powerful current through a lead wire. The wire has a current density so huge that the atoms are destroyed, and the protons and electrons coalesce into pure radiant energy. Relux, under the influence of a magnetic field, converts this directly into electrical potential. Electricity we can convert to the spatial strain in the power coils, and thus the ship is driven." Morey pointed out the huge molecular power cylinder overhead, where the main power drive was located in the inertial center of the ship, or as near as the great space coil would permit.

The smaller power units for vertical lift, and for steering, were in the side walls, hidden under heavy walls of relux.

"The projectors for throwing molecular and heat rays are on the outside of course. Both of these projectors are protected. The walls of the ship are made of an outer wall of heavy lux metal, a vacuum between, and an inner wall of heavy relux. The lux is stronger than relux, and is therefore used for an outer shell. The inner shell of relux will reflect any dangerous rays and serve to hold the heat in the ship, since a perfect reflector is a perfect non-radiator. The vacuum wall is to protect the occupants of the ship against any undue heat. If we should get within the atmosphere of a sun, it would be disastrous if the physical conduction of heat were permitted, for though the relux will turn out any radiated heat, it is a conductor of heat, and we would roast almost instantly. These artificial metals are both absolutely infusible and non-volatile. The ship has actually been in the limb of a star tremendously hotter than your sun or mine.

"Now you see why it is we need not fear a collision with a small sun, meteor or such like. Since we are in our own, artificial space, we are alone, and there is nothing in space to run into. But, if we enter a huge sun, the terrific gravitational field of the mass of matter would be enough to pull the energy of our coil away from us. That actually happened the time we made our first intergalactic exploration. But it is almost impossible to fall into a large star — they are too brilliant. We won't be worrying about it," grinned Morey.

"But how did the ship we captured operate?" asked Zezdon Afthen.

"It was a very ingenious system, very closely related to ours, really.

"We distort space and change the velocity characteristics; in other words, we distort the rate of motion through distance characteristics of normal space. The Thessian ships work on the principle of distorting the rate of progress through time instead of through space.

"*Velocity* is really 'units of travel through space per unit of travel through time.' Now if we make the time unit twice as great, and the units traveled through space are not changed, the *velocity* is twice as great. That is, if we are moving five light years per second, make the second twice as long and we are moving ten light years per double-second. Make it ten thousand times as long, and we are traveling fifty thousand light years per ten-thousand-seconds. This is the principle — but there is a drawback. We might increase the velocity by slowing time passage, that is, if it takes me a year for one heartbeat, two years to raise my arm thus, and six months to turn, my head, if all my body processes are slowed down in this way, I will be able to live a tremendous length of time, and though it takes me two hundred years to go from one star to another, so low is my time rate that the two hundred years will seem but a few minutes. I can then make a trip to a distant star — one five light years distant, let us say, in three minutes to me. I then will say, looking at my chronometer (which has been similarly slowed) 'I have gone five light years in three minutes, or five thirds light years per minute. I have exceeded the speed of light.'

"But people back on Earth would say, he has taken two hundred years to go five light years, therefore he has gone at a speed one fortieth of that of light, which would be true — for their time rate.

"But suppose I can also speed up time. That is, I can live a year in a minute or two. Then everyone else will be exceedingly slow. The ideal thing would be to combine these two effects, arranging that space about your ship will have a very rapid time rate, ten thousand times that of normal space. Then the speed of radiation through that space will be 1,860,000,000 miles per second, and a speed of 1,000,000,000 miles per second would be possible, but still you, too, will be affected, so that though the people back home will say you are going far faster than light, you will say 'No, I am going only 100,000 miles per second.'

"But now imagine that your ship and surrounding space for one mile is at a time rate 10,000 times normal, and you, in a space of one hundred feet within your ship, are affected by a time rate 1/10,000 that, or normal, due to a second, reversing field. The two fields will not fight, or be mutually antagonistic; they will merely compound their effects. Result: you will agree that you are exceeding the speed of light!

"Do you understand? That is the principle on which your ship operated. There were two time-fields, overlapping time-fields. Remember the terrible speed with which your ship landed, and yet there was no appreciable jar according to the men? The answer of course was, that their time rate had been speeded enough, due to the fact that one field had been completely shut off, the other had not.

"That is the principle. The system is so complex, naturally, that we have not yet learned the actual method of working the process. We must do a great deal of mathematical and physical research.

"Wish we had it done — we could use it now," mused the terrestrian.

"We have some other weapons, none as important, of course, as the molecular ray and the heat ray. Or none that have been. But, if the enemy have ray shields, then perhaps these others also will be important. There are molecular motion guns, metal tubes, with molecular director apparatus at one end. A metal shell is pulling the power turned on, and the shell leaps out at a speed of about ten miles per second — since it has been super-heated — and is very accurately aimed, as there is no terrific shock of recoil to be taken up by the gun.

"But a more effective weapon, if these men are as I expect them to be, will be a peculiarly effective magnetic field concentrator device, which will project a magnetic field as a beam for a mile or more. How useful it will be — I don't know. We don't know what the enemy will turn against *us!*"

CHAPTER V

ORTOL

After Morey's explanation of the ship was completed, Wade took Arcot's place at the controls, while Morey and Arcot retired to the calculating room to do some of the needed mathematics on the time-field investigation.

Their work continued here, while the Ortolians prepared a meal and brought it to them, and to Wade. When at last the sun of Ortol was growing before them, Arcot took over controls from Wade once more. Slowing their speed to less than fifty times that of light, they drove on. The attraction of the giant sun was draining the energy from the coils so rapidly now, that at last Arcot was forced to get into normal space, while the planet was still close to a million miles from them. Morey was showing the Ortolians the operation of the telectroscope and had it trained now on the rapidly approaching planet. The planet was easily enlarged to a point where the features of continents were visible. The magnification was increased till cities were no longer blurs, but truly cities.

Suddenly, as city after city was brought under the action of the machine, the Ortolians recognizing them with glad exclamations, one swept into view — and as they watched, it leapt into the air, a vast column of dust, then twisting, whirling, it fell back in utter, chaotic ruin.

Zezdon Fentes staggered back from the screen in horror.

"Arcot — drive down — increase your speed — the Thessians are there already and have destroyed one city," called Morey sharply. The men secured themselves with heavy belts, as the deep toned hum of the warning echoed through the ship. A moment later they staggered under an acceleration of four gravities. Space was dark for the barest instant of time, and then there was the scream of atmosphere as the ship rocketed through the air of the planet at nearly fifteen hundred miles per second. The outer wall was blazing in incandescence in a moment, and the heavy relux screens seemed to leap into place over the windows as the blasting heat, radiated from the incandescent walls flooded in. The millions of tons pressure of the air on the nose of the ship would have brought it to a stop in an instant, and had it not been that the molecular drive was on at full power, driving the ship against the air resistance, and still losing. The ship slowed swiftly, but was shrieking toward the destroyed city at terrific speed.

"Hesthis — to the — right and ahead. That would be their next attack," said the Ortolian. Arcot altered the ship's course, and they shot toward the distance city of Hesthis. They were slowing perceptibly, and yet, though the city was half around the world, they reached it in half a minute. Now Arcot's wizardry at the controls came into play, for by altering his space field constants, he succeeded in reaching a condition that slowed the ship almost instantly to a speed of but a mile a second, yet without apparent deceleration.

High in the white Ortolian sky was a shining point bearing down on the now-visible city. Arcot slanted toward it, and the approaching ship grew like an expanding rubber balloon.

A ray of intense, blindingly brilliant light flashed out, and a gout of light appeared in the center of the city. A huge flame, bright blue, shot heavenward in roaring heat.

Seeing that a strange ship had arrived was enough for the Thessians, and they turned, and drove at Arcot instantly. The Thessian ship was built for a heavy world, and for heavy acceleration in consequence, and, as they had found from the captured ship, it was stronger than the *Ancient Mariner*. Now the Thessians were driving at Arcot with an acceleration and speed that convinced him dodging was useless. Suddenly space was black around them, the sunlit world was gone.

"Wonder what they thought of *that*!" grinned Arcot. Wade smiled grimly.

"It's not what they thought, but what they'll do, that counts."

Arcot came back to normal space, just in time to see the Thessian ship spin in a quick turn, under an acceleration that would have crushed a human to a pulp. Again the pilot dived at the terrestrian ship. Again it vanished. Twice more he tried these fruitless tactics, seeing the ship loom before him — bracing for the crash — then it was gone instantaneously, and though he sailed through the spot he knew it to have occupied, it was not there. Yet an instant later, as he turned, it was floating, unharmed, exactly where his ship had passed!

Rushing was useless. He stood, and prepared to give battle. A molecular ray reached out — and disappeared in flaring ions on a shield utterly impenetrable in the ionizing atmosphere.

Arcot meanwhile watched the instrument of his shield. The Thessian shield would have been impenetrable, but his shield, fed by less efficient tubes, was not, and he knew it. Already the terrific energy of the Thessian ray was noticeably heating the copper plates of the tube. The seal would break soon.

Another ray reached out, a ray of flaring light. Arcot, watching through the "eyes" of his telectroscope viewplates, saw it for but an instant, then the "eyes" were blasted, and the screen went blank.

"He won't do anything with that but burn out eyes," muttered the terrestrian. He pushed a small button when his instruments told him the rays were off. Another scanner came into action, and the viewplate was alive again.

Arcot shot out a cosmic ray himself, and swept the Thessian with it thoroughly. For the instant he needed the enemy ship was blinded. Immediately the *Ancient Mariner* dove, and the automatic ray-finders could no longer hold the rays on his ship. As soon as he was out of the deadly molecular ray he shut off his screen, and turned on all his molecular rays. The Thessian ship, their own ray on, had been unable to put up their screen, as Arcot was unable to use his ray with the enemy's ray forcing him to cover with a shield.

Almost at once the relux covering of the Thessian ship shone with characteristic iridescence as it changed swiftly to lux metal. The molecular ray blinked out, and a ray screen flashed out instead. The Thessians were covering up. Their own rays were useless now. Though Arcot could not hope to destroy their ray shield, they could no longer attack his, for their rays were useless, and already they had lost so much of the protective relux, that they would not be so foolhardy as to risk a second attack of the ray.

Arcot continued to bathe the ship in energy, keeping their "eyes" closed. As long as he could hold his barrage on them, they would not damage him.

"Morey — get into the power room, strap onto the board. Throw all the power-coil banks into the magnets. I may burn them out, but I have hopes —" Arcot already had the generators going full power, charging the power coils.

Morey dived. Almost simultaneously the Thessians succeeded in the maneuver they had been attempting for some time. There were a dozen rays flaring wildly from the ship, searching blindly over the sky and ground, hoping to stumble on the enemy ship, while their own ship dived and twisted. Arcot was busily dodging the sweeping rays, but finally one hit his viewplates, and his own ship was blind. Instantly he threw the ray screen out, cutting off his own molecular ray. His own cosmics he set rotating in cones that covered the three dimensions — save below, where the city lay. Immediately the Thessian had retreated to this one segment where Arcot did not dare throw his own rays. The Thessian cosmics continued to make his relux screens necessary, and his ship remained blind.

His ray screen was showing signs of weakening. The Thessians got a third ray into position for operation, and opened up. Almost at once the tubes heated terrifically. In an instant they would give way. Arcot threw his ship into space, and let the tubes cool under the water jacket. Morey reported the coils ready as soon as he came out of space.

Arcot cut in the new set of eyes, and put up his molecular ray screen again. Then he cut the energy back to the coils.

Half a mile below the enemy ship was vainly scurrying around an empty sky. Wade laughed at the strange resemblance to a puppy chasing its tail. The *Ancient Mariner* was utterly lost to them.

"Well, here goes the last trick," said Arcot grimly. "If this doesn't work, they'll probably win, for their tubes are better than ours, and they can maneuver faster. By win I mean force us to let them attack Ortol. They can't really attack us; artificial space is a perfect defense."

Arcot's molecular ray apprized the Thessians of his presence. Their screen flared up once more. Arcot was driving straight toward their ship as they turned. He snapped the relux screens in front of his eyes an instant before the enemy cosmics reached his ship. Immediately the thud of four heavy relays rang through the ship. The quarter of a million ton ship leaped forward under a terrific acceleration, and then, as the four relays cut out again, the acceleration was gone. The screen regained life as Arcot opened the shutters. Before them, still directly in their path, was the huge Thessian ship. But now its screen was down, the relux iridescent in decomposition. It was falling, helplessly falling to the rocky plateau seven miles below. Its rays reached out even yet — and again the *Ancient Mariner* staggered under the terrific pull of some acceleration. The Thessian ship lurched upward, and a terrific concussion came, and the entire neighborhood of that projector disappeared in a flash of radiation.

Arcot drove the *Ancient Mariner* down beneath the Thessian ship in its long fall, and with a powerful molecular beam ripped a mighty chasm in the deserted plateau. The Thessian ship fell into a quarter mile rift in the solid rock, smashing its way through falling débris. A moment later it was buried beneath a quarter mile of broken rock as Arcot swept a molecular beam about with the grace of a mine foreman filling breaks.

An instant later, a heat ray followed the molecular in dazzling brilliance. A terrific gout of light appeared in the barren rocks. In ten minutes the plateau was a white hot cauldron of molten rocks, glowing now against a darkening sky. Night was falling.

"That ship," said Arcot with an air of finality, "will never rise again."

CHAPTER VI

THE SECOND MOVE

"What happened to him, though?" asked Wade, bewildered. "I haven't yet figured it out. He went down in a heap, and he didn't have any power. Of course, if he had his power he could have pulled out again. He could just melt and burn all the excess rock off, and he would be all set. But his rays all went dead. And why the explosion?"

"The magnetic beam is the answer. In our boat we have everything magnetically shielded, because of the enormous magnetic flux set up by the current flowing from the storage coils to the main coil. But — with so many wires heavily charged with current, what would have happened if they had not been shielded?"

"If a current cuts across a magnetic field, a side thrust is developed. What do you suppose happened when the terrific magnetic field of the beam and the currents in the wires of their powerboard were mutually opposed?"

"Lord, it must have ripped away everything in the ship. It'd tear loose even the lighting wires!" gasped Wade in amazement.

"But if all the power of the ship was destroyed in this way, how was it that one of their rays was operating as they fell?" asked Zezdon Afthen.

"Each ray is a power plant in itself," explained Arcot, "and so it was able to function. I do not know the cause of the explosion, though it might well have been that they had light-bombs such as the Kaxorians of Venus have," he added, thoughtfully.

They landed, at Zezdon's advice, in the city that their arrival had been able to save. This was Ortol's largest city, and their industrial capital. Here, too, was the University at which Afthen taught.

They landed, and Arcot, Morey and Wade, with the aid of Zezdon Afthen and Zezdon Fentes worked steadily for two of their days of fifty hours each, teaching men how to make and use the molecular ships, and the rays and screens, heat beams, and relux. But Arcot promised that when he returned he would have some weapon that would bring them certain and easy salvation. In the meantime other terrestrians would follow him.

They left the morning of their third day on the planet. A huge crowd had come to cheer them on their way as they left, but it was the "silent cheer" of Ortol, a telepathic well-wishing.

"Now," said Arcot as their ship left the planet behind, "we will have to make the next move. It certainly looks as though that next move would be to the still-unknown race that lives on world 3769-37, 478, 326, 894-6. Evidently we will have to have some weapon they haven't, and I think that I know what it will be. Thanks to our trip out to the Islands of Space."

"Shall we go?"

"I think it would be wise," agreed Morey.

"And I," said Wade. The Ortolians agreed, and so, with the aid of the photographic copies of the Thessian charts that Arcot had made, they started for world 3769-37, 478, 326, 894-6.

"It will take approximately twenty-two hours, and as we have been putting off our sleep with drugs, I think that we had better catch up. Wade, I wish you'd take the ship again, while Morey and I do a little concentrated sleeping. We have by no means finished that calculation, and I'd very much like to. We'll relieve you in five hours."

Wade took the ship, and following the course Arcot laid out, they sped through the void at the greatest safe speed. Wade had only to watch the view-screen carefully, and if a star showed as growing rapidly, it was proof that they were near, and nearing rapidly. If large, a touch of a switch, and they dodged to one side, if small, they were suddenly plunged into an instant of unbelievable radiation as they swept through it, in a different space, yet linked to it by radiation, not light, that were permitted in.

Zezdon Afthen had elected to stay with him, which gave him an opportunity he had been waiting for. "If it's none of my business, just say so," he began. "But that first city we saw the Thessians destroy — it was Zezdon Fentes' home, wasn't it? Did he have a family?"

The words seemed blunt as he said them, but there was no way out, once he had started. And Zezdon Afthen took the question with complete calm.

"Fentes had both wives and children," he said quietly. "His loss was great."

Wade concentrated on the screen for a moment, trying to absorb the shock. Then, fearing Zezdon Afthen might misinterpret his silence, he plunged on. "I'm sorry," he said. "I didn't realize you were polygamous — most people on Earth aren't, but some groups are. It's probably a good way to improve the race. But . . . Blast it, what bothers me is that Zezdon Fentes seemed to recover from the blow so quickly! From a canine race, I'd expect more affection, more loyalty, more. . . ."

He stopped in dismay. But Zezdon Afthen remained unperturbed. "More unconcealed emotion?" he asked. "No. Affection and loyalty we have — they *are* characteristic of our race. But affection and loyalty should not be uselessly applied. To *forget* dead wives and children — that would be insulting to their memory. But to mourn them with senseless loss of health and balance would also be insulting — not only to their memory, but to the entire race.

"No, we have a better way. Fentes, my very good friend, has not forgotten, no more than you have forgotten the death of your mother, whom you loved. But you no longer mourn her death with a fear and horror of that natural thing, the Eternal Sleep. Time has softened the pain.

"If we can do the same in five minutes instead of five years, is it not better? That is why Fentes has *forgotten*".

"Then you have aged his memory of that event?" asked Wade in surprise.

"That is one way of stating it," replied Zezdon Afthen seriously.

Wade was silent for a while, absorbing this. But he could not contain his curiosity completely. *Well, to hell with it,* he decided. *Conventional manners and tact don't have much meaning between two different races.* "Are you — married?" he asked.

"Only three times," Zezdon Afthen told him blandly. "And to forestall your next question — no, our system does not create problems. At least, not those you're thinking of. I know my wives have never had the jealous quarrels I see in your mind pictures."

"It isn't safe thinking things around you," laughed Wade. "Just the same, all of this has made me even more interested in the 'Ancient Masters' you keep mentioning. Who were they?"

"The Ancient Ones," began Zezdon Afthen slowly, "were men such as you are. They descended from a primeval omnivorous mammal very closely related to your race. Evidently the tendency of evolution on any planet is approximately the same with given conditions.

"The race existed as a distinct branch for approximately 1,500,000 of your years before any noticeable culture was developed. Then it existed for a total of 1,525,000 years before extinction. With culture and learning they developed such marvelous means of killing themselves that in twenty-five thousand years they succeeded perfectly. Ten thousand years of barbaric culture — I need not relate it to you, five thousand years of the medieval culture, then five thousand years of developed science culture.

"They learned to fly through space and nearly populated three worlds; two were fully populated, one was still under colonization when the great war broke out. An interplanetary war is not a long drawn out struggle. The science of any people so far advanced as to have interplanetary lines is too far developed to permit any long duration of war. Selto declared war, and made the first move. They attacked and destroyed the largest city of Ortol of that time. Ortolian ships drove them off, and in turn attacked Selto's largest city. Twenty million intelligences, twenty million lives, each with its aims, its hopes, its loves and its strivings — gone in four days.

"The war continued to get more and more hateful, till it became evident that neither side would be pacified till the other was totally subjugated. So each laid his plans, and laid them to wipe out the entire world of the other.

"Ortol developed a ray of light that made things not happen," explained Zezdon Afthen, his confused thoughts clearly indicating his own uncertainty.

"'A ray of light that made things not happen,'" repeated Wade curiously. "A ray, which prevented things, which caused processes to stop — *The Negrian Death Ray!*" he exclaimed as he suddenly recognized, in this crude and garbled description of its powers, the Negrian ray of anti-catalysis, a ray which tended to stop the processes of life's chemistry and bring instant, painless death.

"Ah, you know it, too?" asked the Ortolian eagerly. "Then you will understand what happened. The ray was turned first on Selto, and as the whirling planet spun under it, every square foot of it was wiped clean of every living thing, from gigantic Welsthan to microscopic Ascoptel, and every man, woman and child was killed, painlessly, but instantly.

"Then Thenten spun under it, and all were killed, but many who had fled the planets were still safe — many? — a few thousand.

"The day that Thenten spun under that ray, men of Ortol began to complain of disease — men by the thousands, hundreds of thousands. Every man, every woman, every child was afflicted in some way. The diseases did not seem all the same. Some seemingly died of a disease of the lungs, some went insane, some were paralyzed, and lay helplessly inactive. But most of them were afflicted, for it was exceedingly virulent, and the normal serums were helpless. Before any quantity of new serum was made, all but a slender remnant had died, either of starvation through paralysis, none being left to care for them, or from the disease itself, while thousands who had gone mad were painlessly killed.

"The Seltonians came to Ortol, and the remaining Ortolians, with their aid, tried to rebuild the civilization. But what a sorry thing! The cities were gigantic, stinking, plague-ridden morgues. And the plague broke among those few remaining people. The Ortolians had done everything in their power with the serums — but too late. The Seltonians had been protected with it on landing — but even that was not enough. Again the wild fires of that loathsome disease broke out.

"Since first those men had developed from their hairy forebears, they had found their eternal friends were the dogs, and to them they turned in their last extremity, breeding them for intelligence, hairlessness, and resemblance to themselves. The Deathless ones alone remained after three generations of my people, but with the aid of certain rays, the rays capable of penetrating lead for a short distance, and most other substances for considerable distances." X-rays, thought Wade. "Great changes had been wrought. Already they had developed startling intelligence, and were able to understand the scheme of their Masters. Their feet and hands were being modified rapidly, and their vocal apparatus was changing. Their jaws shortened, their chins developed, the nose retreated.

"Generation after generation the process went on, while the Deathless Ancient Ones worked with their helpers, for soon my race was a real helping organization.

"But it was done. The successful arousing of true love-emotion followed, and the unhappy days were gone. Quickly development followed. In five thousand years the new race had outstripped the Ancient Masters, and they passed, voluntarily, willingly joining in oblivion the millions who had died before.

"Since then our own race has risen, it has been but a short thousand years, a thousand years of work, and hope, and continuous improvement for us, continual accomplishment on which we can look, and a living hope to which we could look with raised heads, and smiling faces.

"Then our hope died, as this menace came. Do you see what you and your world was meant to us, Man of Earth?" Zezdon Afthen raised his dark eyes to the terrestrian with a look in their depths that made Wade involuntarily resolve that Thet and all Thessians should be promptly consigned to that limbo of forgotten things where they belonged.

CHAPTER VII

WORLD 3769-37,478,326,894,6, TALSO

Wade sat staring moodily at the screen for some time, while Zezdon Afthen, sunk in his own reveries, continued.

"Our race was too highly psychic, and too little mechanically curious. We learned too little of the world about, and too much of our own processes. We are a peaceful race, for, while you and the Ancient Masters learned the rule of existence in a world of strife, where only the fittest, the best fighters survived, we learned life in a carefully tended world, where the Ancient Masters taught us to live, where the one whose social instincts were best developed, where he who would most help the others, and the race, was permitted to live. Is it not natural that our race will not fight among themselves? We are careful to suppress tendencies toward criminality and struggle. The criminal and the maniac, or those who are permanently incurable as determined by careful examination, are 'removed' as the Leaders put it. Lethal gas.

"At any rate, we know so pitiably little of natural science. We were hopelessly helpless against an attacking science."

"I promise you, Afthen, that if Earth survives, Ortol shall survive, for we have given you all the weapons we know of and we will give your people all the weapons we shall learn of." Morey spoke from the doorway. Arcot was directly behind him.

They talked for a short while, then Wade retired for some needed sleep, while Morey and Arcot started further work on the time fields.

Hour after hour the ship sped on through the dark of space, weirdly distorted, glowing spots of light before them, wheeling suns that moved and flashed as their awesome speed whirled them on.

They had to move slower soon, as the changing stars showed them near the space-marks of certain locating suns. Finally, still moving close to fifteen thousand miles per second, they saw the sun they knew was sun 3769-37,478,-326,894, twice as large as Sol, two and a half times as massive and twenty-six times as brilliant.

Thirteen major planets they counted as they searched the system with their powerful telectroscope, the outermost more than ten billion miles from the parent sun, while planet six, the one indicated by the world number, was at a distance of five hundred million miles, nearly as far from the sun as Jupiter is from ours, yet the giant sun, giving more than twenty-five times as much heat and light in the blue-white range, heated the planet to approximately the same temperature Earth enjoys. Spectroscopy showed that the atmosphere was well supplied with oxygen, and so the inhabitants were evidently oxygen-breathing men, unlike those of the Negrian people who live in an atmosphere of hydrogen.

Arcot threw the ship toward the planet, and as it loomed swiftly larger, he shut off the space-control, and set the coils for full charge, while the ship entered the planet's atmosphere in a screaming dive, still at a speed of better than a hundred miles a second. But this speed was quickly damped as the ship shot high over broad oceans to the dull green of land ahead in the daylit zone. Observations made from various distances by means of the space-control, thus going back in time, show that the planet had a day of approximately forty hours, the diameter was nearly nine thousand miles, which would probably mean an inconveniently high gravity for the terrestrians and a distressingly high gravity for the Ortolians, used to their world even smaller than Earth, with scarcely 80 percent of Earth's gravity.

Wade made some volumetric analysis of the atmosphere, and with the aid of a mouse, pronounced it "Q.A.R." (quite all right) for human beings. It had not killed the mouse, so probably humans would find it quite all right.

"We'll land at the first city that comes into view," suggested Arcot. "Afthen, you be the spokesman; you have a very considerable ability with the mental communication, and have a better understanding of the physics we need to explain than has Zezdon Fentes."

They were over land, a rocky coast that shot behind them as great jagged mountains, tipped with snow, rose beneath. Suddenly, a shining apparition appeared from behind one of the neighboring hills, and drove down at them with an unearthly acceleration. Arcot moved just enough to dodge the blow, and turned to meet the ship. Instantly, now that he had a good view of it he was certain it was a Thessian ship. Waiting no longer to determine that it was not a ship of this world, he shot a molecular beam at it. The beam exploded into a coruscating panoply of pyrotechnics on the Thessian shield. The Thessian replied with all beams he had available, including an induction-beam, an intensely brilliant light-beam, and several molecular cannons with shells loaded with an explosive that was very evidently condensed light. This was no exploration ship, but a full-fledged battleship.

The *Ancient Mariner* was blinded instantly. None of the occupants were hurt, but the combined pressure of the various beams hurled the ship to one side. The induction beam alone was dangerous. It passed through the outer lux-metal wall unhindered, and the perfectly conducting relux wall absorbed it, and turned it into power. At once, all the metal objects in the ship began to heat up with terrific rapidity. Since there were no metallic conductors on the ship, no damage was done.

Arcot immediately hid behind his perfect shield — the space-distortion.

"That's no mild dose," he said in a tense voice, working rapidly. "He's a real-for-sure battleship. Better get down in the power room, Morey."

In a few moments the ship was ready again. Opening the shield somewhat, Arcot was able to determine that no rays were being played on it, for no energy fields disclosed as distorting the opened field, other than the field of the sun and planet.

Arcot opened it. The battleship was searching vainly about the mountains, and was now some miles distant. His last view of Arcot's ship had been a suddenly contracting ship, one that vanished in infinite distance, the infinite distance of another space, though he did not know it.

Arcot turned three powerful heat beams on the Thessian ship, and drove down toward it, accompanying them with molecular rays. The Thessian shield stopped the moleculars, but the heat had already destroyed the eyes of the ship. By some system of magnetic or electrostatic locating devices, the enemy guns and rays replied, and so successfully that Arcot was again blinded.

He had again been driving in a line straight toward the enemy, and now he threw in the entire power of his huge magnetic field-rays. The induction ray disappeared, and the heat, light and cannons stopped.

"Worked again," grinned Arcot. A new set of eyes was inserted automatically, and the screen again lighted. The Thessian ship was spinning end over end toward the ground. It landed with a tremendous crash. Simultaneously from the rear of the *Ancient Mariner* came a terrific crash, an explosion that drove the terrestrial ship forward, as though a giant hand had pushed it from behind.

The *Ancient Mariner* spun like a top, facing the direction of the explosion, though still traveling in the direction it had been pursuing, but backward now. Behind them the air was a gigantic pool of ionization. Tremendous fragments of what obviously had been a ship were drifting down, turning end over end. And those fragments of the wall showed them to be fully four feet of solid relux.

"Enemy got up behind somehow while the eyes were out, and was ready to raise merry hell. Somebody blew them up beautifully. Look at the ground down there — it's red hot. That's from the radiated heat of our recent encounter. Heat rays reflected, light bombs turned off, heat escaping from ions — nice little workout — and it didn't seriously bother our defenses of two-inch relux. Now tell me: what will blow up four-foot relux?" asked Arcot, looking at the fragments. "It seems to me those fellows don't need any help from us; they may decline it with thanks."

"But they may be willing to help us," replied Afthen, "and we certainly need such help."

"I didn't expect to come out alive from that battleship there. It was luck. If they knew what we had, they could insulate against it in an hour," added Arcot.

"Let's finish those fellows over there — look!" From the wreck of the ship they had downed, a stream of men in glistening relux suits were filing. Any men comparable to humans would have been killed by the fall, but not Thessians. They carried peculiar machines, and as they drove out of the ship in dive that looked as though they had been shot from a cannon, they turned and landed on the ground and proceeded to jump back, leaping at a speed that was bewildering, seemingly impossible in any living creature.

They busied themselves quickly. It took less than thirty seconds, and they had a large relux disc laid under the entire group and machines. Arcot turned a molecular ray down. The rock and soil shot up all about them, even the ship shot up, to fall back into the great pit its ray had formed. But the ionization told of the ray shield over the little group of men. A heat ray reached down, while the men still frantically worked at their stubby projectors. The relux disc now showed its purpose. In an instant the soil about them was white hot, bubbling lava. It was liquid, boiling furiously. But the deep relux disc simply floated on it. The enemy ship began sinking, and in a moment had fallen almost completely beneath the white hot rock.

A fountain of the melted lava sprung up, and under Arcot's skillful direction, fell in a cloud of molten rock on the men working. The suits protected, and the white hot stuff simply rolled off. But it was sinking their boat. Arcot continued hopefully.

Meanwhile a signaling machine was frantically calling for help and sending out information of their plight and position.

Then all was instantly wiped out in a single terrific jolt of the magnetic beam. The machines jumped a little, despite their weight, and the ray shield apparatus slumped suddenly in blazing white heat, the interior mechanism fused. But the men were still active, and rapidly spreading from the spot, each protected by a ray shield pack.

A brilliant stab of molecular ray shot at each from either of two of the *Ancient Mariner*'s projectors as Morey aided Arcot. Their little packs flared brilliantly for an instant under the thousands of horsepower of energy lashing at the screen, then flashed away, and the opalescent relux yielded a moment later, and the figure went twisting, hurtling away. Meanwhile Wade was busy with the magnetic apparatus, destroying shield after shield, which either Arcot or Morey picked off. The fall from even so much as half a mile seemed not sufficient to seriously bother these supermen, for an instant later they would be up tearing away in great leaps on their own power as their molecular suits, blown out by the magnetic field, failed them.

It was but a matter of minutes before the last had been chased down either by the rays or the ship. Then, circling back, Arcot slowly settled beside the enemy ship.

"Wait," called Arcot sharply as Morey started for the door.

"Don't go out yet. The friends who wrecked that little sweetheart who crept up behind will probably show up. Wait and see what happens." Hardly had he spoken, when a strange apparition rose from behind a rock scarcely a quarter of a mile away. Immediately Arcot intensified the vision screen covering him. He seemed to leap near. There was one man, and he held what was obviously a sword by the blade, above his head, waving it from side to side.

"There they are — whatever they are. Intelligent all right — what more universally obvious peace sign than a primitive weapon such as a knife held in reverse position? You go with Zezdon Afthen. Try holding a carving knife by the blade."

Morey grinned as he got into his power suit, on Wade's O.K. of the atmosphere. "They may mistake me for the cook out looking for dinner, and I wouldn't risk my dignity that way. I'll take the baseball bat and hold it wrong way instead."

Nevertheless, as he stepped from the ship, with Afthen close behind, he held the long knife by the blade, and Afthen, very awkwardly operating his still rather unfamiliar power suit, followed.

Into the intensely blue sunlight the men stepped. Their skin and clothing took on a peculiar tint under the strange sunlight.

The single stranger was joined by a second, also holding a reversed weapon, and together they threw them down. Morey and Zezdon Afthen followed suit. The two parties advanced toward each other.

The strangers advanced with a swift, light step, jumping from rock to rock, while Morey and Afthen flew part way toward them. The men of this world were totally unlike any intelligent race Morey had conceived of. Their head and brain case was so small as to be almost animalish. The nose was small and well formed, the ears more or less cup-shaped with a remarkable power of motion. Their eyes were seemingly huge, probably no larger than a terrestrian's, though in the tiny head they were necessarily closely placed, protected by heavy bony ridges that actually projected from the skull to enclose them. Tiny, childlike chins completed the head, running down to a scrawny neck.

They were short, scarcely five feet, yet evidently of tremendous strength for their short, heavy arms, the muscle bulging plainly under the tight rubber-like composition garments, and the short legs whose stocky girth proclaimed equal strength were members of a body in keeping with them. The deep, broad chest, wide, square shoulders, heavy broad hips, combined with the tiny head seemed to indicate a perfect incarnation of brainless, brute strength.

"Strangers from another planet, enemies of our enemies. What brings you here at this time of troubles?" The thoughts came clearly from the stocky individual before them.

"We seek to aid, and to find aid. The menace that you face, attacks not alone your world, but all this star cluster," replied Zezdon Afthen steadily.

The stranger shook his head with an evident expression of hopelessness. "The menace is even greater than we feared. It was just fortune that permitted us to have our weapon in workable condition at the time your ship was attacked. It will be a day before the machine will again be capable of successful operation. When in condition for use, it is invincible, but — one blow in thirty hours — you can see we are not of great aid." He shrugged.

An enemy with evident resources of tremendous power, deadly, unknown rays that wiped out entire cities with a single brief sweep — and no defense save this single weapon, good but once a day! Morey could read the utter despair of the man.

"What is the difficulty?" asked Morey eagerly.

"Power, lack of power. Our cities are going without power, while every electric generator on the planet is pouring its output into the accumulators that work these damnable, hopeless things. Invincible with power — helpless without."

"Ah!" Morey's face shone with delight — invincible weapon — with power. And the *Ancient Mariner* could generate unthinkable power.

"What power source do you use — how do you generate your power?"

"Combining oxidizing agent with reducing agents releases heat. Heat used to boil liquid and the vapor runs turbines."

"We can give you power. What wattage have you available?"

Only Morey's thoughts had to translate "watts" to "How many man-weights can you lift through your height per time interval, equal to this." He gave the man some impression of a second, by counting. The man figured rapidly. His answer indicated that approximately a total of two billion kilowatts were available.

"Then the weapon is invincible hereafter, if what you say is true. Our ship alone can easily generate ten thousand times that power.

"Come, get in the ship, accompany us to your capital."

The men turned, and retreated to their position behind the rocks, while Morey and Zezdon Afthen waited for them. Soon they returned, and entered the ship.

"Our world," explained the leader rapidly, "is a single unified colony. The capital is 'Shesto,' our world we call 'Talso.'" His directions were explicit, and Arcot started for Shesto, on Talso.

CHAPTER VIII

UNDEFEATABLE OR UNCONTROLLABLE?

Fifteen minutes after they started, they came to Shesto. They were forced to land, and explain, for their relux ship was decidedly not the popular Talsonian idea of a life-saver.

Shesto was defended by two of the machines, and each machine had been equipped with two fully charged accumulators. Their four possible shots were hoped to be sufficient protection, and, so far, had been. The city had been attacked twice, according to Tho Stan Drel, the Talsonian: once by a single ship which had been instantly destroyed, and once by a fleet of six ships. The interval had permitted time to recharge the discharged accumulator, and the fleet had been badly treated. Of the six ships, four had been brought down in rapid succession, and the remaining two ships had fled.

When the first city had been wiped out, with a loss of life well in the hundreds of thousands, the other cities had, to limit of their abilities, set up the protective apparatus. Apparently the Thessians were holding off for the present.

"In a way," said Morey seriously, "it was distinctly fortunate that we were attacked almost at once. Their instantaneous system of destruction would have worked for the one shot needed to send the *Ancient Mariner* to eternal blazes." He laughed, but it was a slightly nervous laugh.

The terrestrial ship landed in a great grassy court, and out of respect for the parklike smoothness of the turf, Arcot left the ship on its power units, suspended a bit above the surface. Then he, Morey and the Talsonian left the ship. Zezdon Afthen was left with the ship and with Wade in charge, for if some difficulties were encountered, Wade would be able to help them with the ship, and Zezdon Afthen with the tremendous power of his thought locating apparatus, was busy seeking out the Thessian stronghold.

A party of men of Talso met the terrestrians outside the ship.

"Welcome, Men of another world, and to you go our thanks for the destruction of one of our enemies." The clear thoughts of the spokesman evinced his ability to concentrate.

"And to your world must go our thanks for saving of our lives, and more important, our ship," replied Arcot. "For the ship represents a thing of enormous value to this entire star-system."

"I see — understand — your — thoughts that you wish to learn more of this weapon we use. You understand that it is a question among us as to whether it is undefeatable, uncontrollable or just un-understandable. We have had fair success with it. It is not a weapon, was not developed as such; it was an experiment in the line of electric-waves. How it works, what it is, what happens — we do not know.

"But men who can create so marvelous a ship as this of yours, capable of destroying a ship of the Thessians with their own weapons must certainly be able to understand any machine we may make — and you have power?" he finished eagerly.

"Practically infinite power. I will throw into any power line you suggest, all the direct current you wish." Arcot's thoughts were pure reflection, but the Talsonian brightened at once.

"I feared it might be alternating — but we can handle direct current. All our transmission is done at high voltage direct current. What potential do you generate? Will we have to install changers?"

"We generate D.C. at any voltage up to fifty million, any power up to that needed to lift ten trillion men through their own height in this time a second." The power represented approximately twenty trillion horsepower.

The Talsonian's face went blank with amazement as he looked at the ship. "In that tiny thing you generate such power?" he asked in amazement.

"In that tiny ship we generate more than one million times that power," Arcot said.

"Our power troubles are over," declared the military man emphatically.

"Our troubles are not over," replied a civilian who had joined the party, with equal emphasis. "As a matter of fact, they are worse than ever. More tantalizing. What he says means that we have a tremendous power source, but it is in one spot. How are you going to transmit the power? We can't possibly move any power anywhere near that amount. We couldn't touch it to our lines without having them all go up in one instantaneous blaze of glory.

"We cannot drain such a lake of power through our tiny power pipes of silver."

"This man is Stel Felso Theu," said Tho Stan Drel. "The greatest of our scientists, the man who has invented this weapon which alone seems to offer us hope. And I am afraid he is right. See, there is the University. For the power requirements of their laboratories, a heavy power line has been installed, and it was hoped that you could carry leads into it." His face showed evident despair greater than ever.

"We can always feed some power into the lines. Let us see just what hope there is. I think that it would be wiser to investigate the power lines at once," suggested Morey.

Ten minutes later, with but a single officer now accompanying them, Tho Stan Drel, the terrestrial scientist, and the Talsonian scientist were inspecting the power installation.

They had entered a large stone building, into which led numerous very heavy silver wires. The insulators were silicate glass. Their height suggested a voltage of well over one hundred thousand, and such heavy cables suggested a very heavy amperage, so that a tremendous load was expected.

Within the building were a series of gigantic glass tubes, their walls fully three inches thick, and even so, braced with heavy platinum rods. Inside the tubes were tremendous elements such as the tiny tubes of their machine carried. Great cables led into them, and now their heating coils were glowing a somberly deep red.

Along the walls were the switchboards, dozens of them, all sizes, all types of instruments, strange to the eyes of the terrestrians, and in practically all the light-beam indicator system was used, no metallic pointers, but tiny mirrors directing a very fine line of brilliant light acted as a needle. The system thus had practically no inertia.

"Are these the changers?" asked Arcot gazing at the gigantic tubes.

"They are; each tube will handle up to a hundred thousand volts," said Stel Felso Theu.

"But I fear, Stel Felso Theu, that these tubes will carry power only one way; that is, it would be impossible for power to be pumped from here into the power house, though the process can be reversed," pointed out Arcot. "Radio tubes work only one way, which is why they can act as rectifiers. The same was true of these tubes. They could carry power one way only."

"True, of tubes in general," replied the Talsonian, "and I see by that that you know the entire theory of our tubes, which is rather abstruse."

"We use them on the ship, in special form," interrupted Arcot.

"Then I will only say that the college here has a very complete electric power plant of its own. On special occasions, the power generated here is needed by the city, and so we arranged the tubes with switches which could reverse the flow. At present they are operating to pour power into the city.

"If your ship can generate such tremendous power, I suspect that it would be wiser to eliminate the tubes from the circuit, for they put certain restrictions on the line. The main power plant in the city has tube banks capable of handling anything the line would. I suggest that your voltage be set at the maximum that the line will carry without breakdown, and the amperage can be made as high as possible without heat loss."

"Good enough. The line to the city power will stand what pressure?"

"It is good for the maximum of these tubes," replied the Talsonian.

"Then get into communication with the city plant and tell them to prepare for every work-unit they can carry. I'll get the generator." Arcot turned, and flew on his power suit to the ship.

In a few moments he was back, a molecular pistol in one hand, and suspended in front of him on nothing but a ray of ionized air, to all appearances, a cylindrical apparatus, with a small cubical base.

The cylinder was about four feet long, and the cubical box about eighteen inches on a side.

"What is that, and what supports it?" asked the Talsonian scientists in surprise.

"The thing is supported by a ray which directs the molecules of a small bar in the top clamp, driving it up," explained Morey, "and that is the generator."

"That! Why it is hardly as big as a man!" exclaimed the Talsonian.

"Nevertheless, it can generate a billion horsepower. But you couldn't get the power away if you did generate it." He turned toward Arcot, and called to him.

"Arcot — set it down and let her rip on about half a million horsepower for a second or so. Air arc. Won't hurt it — she's made of lux and relux."

Arcot grinned, and set it on the ground. "Make an awful hole in the ground."

"Oh — go ahead. It will satisfy this fellow, I think," replied Morey.

Arcot pulled a very thin lux metal cord from his pocket, and attached one end of a long loop to one tiny switch, and the other to a second. Then he adjusted three small dials. The wire in hand, he retreated to a distance of nearly two hundred feet, while Morey warned the Talsonians back. Arcot pulled one end of his cord.

Instantly a terrific roar nearly deafened the men, a solid sheet of blinding flame reached in a flaming cone into the air for nearly fifty feet. The screeching roar continued for a moment, then the heat was so intense that Arcot could stand no more, and pulled the cord. The flame died instantly, though a slight ionization clung briefly. In a moment it had cooled to white, and was cooling slowly through orange — red deep — red —

The grass for thirty feet about was gone, the soil for ten feet about was molten, boiling. The machine itself was in a little crater, half sunk in boiling rock. The Talsonians stared in amazement. Then a sort of sigh escaped them and they started forward. Arcot raised his molecular pistol, a blue green ray reached out, and the rock suddenly was black. It settled swiftly down, and a slight depression was the only evidence of the terrific action.

Arcot walked over the now cool rock, cooled by the action of the molecular ray. In driving the molecules downward, the work was done by the heat of these molecules. The machine was frozen in the solid lava.

"Brilliant idea, Morey," said Arcot disgustedly. "It'll be a nice job breaking it loose."

Morey stuck the lux metal bar in the top clamp, walked off some distance, and snapped on the power. The rock immediately about the machine was molten again. A touch of the molecular pistol to the lux metal bar, and the machine jumped free of the molten rock.

Morey shut off the power. The machine was perfectly clean, and extremely hot.

"And your ship is made of that stuff!" exclaimed the Talsonian scientist. "What will destroy it?"

"Your weapon will, apparently."

"But do you believe that we have power enough?" asked Morey with a smile.

"No — it's entirely too much. Can you tone that condensed lightning bolt down to a workable level?"

CHAPTER IX

THE IRRESISTIBLE AND THE IMMOVABLE

The generator Arcot had brought was one of the two spare generators used for laboratory work. He took it now into the sub-station, and directed the Talsonian students and the scientist in the task of connecting it into the lines; though they knew where it belonged, he knew *how* it belonged.

Then the terrestrian turned on the power, and gradually increased it until the power authorities were afraid of break-downs. The accumulators were charged in the city, and the power was being shipped to other cities whose accumulators were not completely charged.

But, after giving simple operating instructions to the students, Arcot and Morey went with Stel Felso Theu to his laboratory.

"Here," Stel Felso Theu explained, "is the original apparatus. All these other machines you see are but replicas of this. How it works, why it works, even what it does, I am not sure of. Perhaps you will understand it. The thing is fully charged now, for it is, in part, one of the defenses of the city. Examine it now, and then I will show its power."

Arcot looked it over in silence, following the great silver leads with keen interest. Finally he straightened, and returned to the Talsonian. In a moment Morey joined them.

The Talsonian then threw a switch, and an intense ionization appeared within the tube, then a minute spot of light was visible within the sphere of light. The minute spot of radiance is the real secret of the weapon. The ball of fire around it is merely wasted energy.

"Now I will bring it out of the tube." There were three dials on the control panel from which he worked, and now he adjusted one of these. The ball of fire moved steadily toward the glass wall of the tube, and with a crash the glass exploded inward. It had been highly evacuated. Instantly the tiny ball of fire about the point of light expanded to a large globe.

"It is now in the outer air. We make the — thing, in an evacu-ated glass tube, but as they are cheap, it is not an expensive proce-dure. The ball will last in its present condition for approximately three hours. Feel the exceedingly intense heat? It is radiating away its vast energy.

"Now here is the point of greatest interest." Again the

Talsonian fell to work on his dials, watching the ball of fire. It seemed far more brilliant in the air now. It moved, and headed toward a great slab of steel off to one side of the laboratory. It shifted about until it was directly over the center of the great slab. The slab rested on a scale of some sort, and as the ball of fire touched it, the scale showed a sudden increase in load. The ball sank into the slab of steel, and the scale showed a steady, enormous load. Evidently the little ball was pressing its way through as though it were a solid body. In a moment it was through the steel slab, and out on the other side.

"It will pass through any body with equal ease. It seems to answer only these controls, and these it answers perfectly, and without difficulty.

"One other thing we can do with it. I can increase its rate of energy discharge."

The Talsonian turned a fourth dial, well off to one side, and the brilliance of the spot increased enormously. The heat was unbearable. Almost at once he shut it off.

"That is the principle we use in making it a weapon. Watch the actual operation."

The ball of fire shot toward an open window, out the window, and vanished in the sky above. The Talsonian stopped the rotation of the dials. "It is motionless now, but scarcely visible. I will now release all the energy." He twirled the fourth dial, and instantly there was a flash of light, and a moment later a terrific concussion.

"It is gone." He left the controls, and went over to his apparatus. He set a heavy silver bladed switch, and placed a new tube in the apparatus. A second switch arced a bit as he drove it home. "Your generator is recharging the accumulators."

Stel Felso Theu took the backplate of the control cabinet off, and the terrestrians looked at the control with interest.

"Got it, Morey?" asked Arcot after a time.

"Think so. Want to try making it up? We can do so out of spare junk about the ship, I think. We won't need the tube if what I believe of it is true."

Arcot turned to the Talsonian. "We wish you to accompany us to the ship. We have apparatus there which we wish to set up."

Back to the ship they went. There Arcot, Morey and Wade worked rapidly.

It was about three-quarters of an hour later when Arcot and his friends called the others to the laboratory. They had a maze of apparatus on the power bench, and the shining relux conductors ran all over the ship apparently. One huge bar ran into the power room itself, and plugged into the huge power-coil power supply.

They were still working at it, but looked up as the others entered. "Guess it will work," said Arcot with a grin.

There were four dials, and three huge switches. Arcot set all four dials, and threw one of the switches. Then he started slowly turning the fourth dial. In the center of the room a dim, shining mist a foot in diameter began to appear. It condensed, solidified without shrinking, a solid ball of matter a foot in diameter. It seemed black, but was a perfectly reflective surface — and luminous!

"Then — then you had already known of this thing? Then why did you not tell me when I tried to show it?" demanded the Talsonian.

Arcot was sending the globe, now perfectly non-luminous, about the room. It flattened out suddenly, and was a disc. He tossed a small weight on it, and it remained fixed, but began to radiate slightly. Arcot readjusted his dials, and it ceased radiating, held perfectly motionless. The sphere returned, and the weight dropped to the floor. Arcot maneuvered it about for a moment more. Then he placed his friends behind a screen of relux, and increased the radiation of the globe tremendously. The heat became intense, and he stopped the radiation.

"No, Stel Felso Theu, we do not have this on our world," Arcot said.

"You do not have it! You look at my apparatus fifteen minutes, and then work for an hour — and you have apparatus far more effective than ours, which required years of development!" exclaimed the Talsonian.

"Ah, but it was not wholly new to me. This ship is driven by curving space into peculiar coordinates. Even so, we didn't do such a hot job, did we, Morey?"

"No, we should have —"

"What — it was not a good job?" interrupted the Talsonian. "You succeeded in creating it in air — in making it stop radiating, in making a ball a foot in diameter, made it change to a disc, made it carry a load — what do you want?"

"We want the full possibilities, the only thing that can save us in this war," Morey said.

"What you learned how to do was the reverse of the process we learned. How you did it is a wonder — but you did. Very well — matter is energy — does your physics know that?" asked Arcot.

"It does; matter contains vast energy," replied the Talsonian.

"Matter has mass, and energy because of that! Mass *is* energy. Energy in any known form is a field of force in space. So matter is ordinarily a combination of magnetic, electrostatic and gravitational fields. Your apparatus combined the three, and put them together. The result was — matter!

"You created matter. We can destroy it but we cannot create it.

"What we ordinarily call matter is just a marker, a sign that there are those energy-fields. Each bit is surrounded by a gravitational field. The bit is just the marker of that gravitational field.

"But that seems to be wrong. This artificial matter of yours seems also a sort of knot, for you make all three fields, combine them, and have the matter, but not, very apparently, like normal matter. Normal matter also holds the fields that make it. The artificial matter is surrounded by the right fields, but it is evidently not able to hold the fields, as normal matter does. That was why your matter continually disintegrated to ordinary energy. The energy was not bound properly.

"But the reason why it would blow up so was obvious. It did not take much to destroy the slight hold that the artificial matter had on its field, and then it instantly proceeded to release all its energy at once. And as you poured millions of horsepower into it all day to fill it, it naturally raised merry hell when it let loose."

Arcot was speaking eagerly, excitedly.

"But here is the great fact, the important thing: It is artificially created in a given place. It is made, and exists at the point determined by these three coordinated dials. It is not natural, and can exist only where it is made and nowhere else — obvious, but important. It cannot exist save at the point designated. Then, if that point moves along a line, the artificial matter must follow that moving point and be always at that point. Suppose now that a slab of steel is on that line. The point moves to it — through it. To exist, that artificial matter *must* follow it through the steel — if not, it is destroyed. Then the steel is attempting to destroy the artificial matter. If the matter has sufficient energy, it will force the steel out of the way, and penetrate. The same is true of any other matter, lux metal or relux — it will penetrate. To continue in existence it must. And it has great energy, and will expend every erg of that energy of existence to continue existence.

"It is, as long as its energy holds out, absolutely irresistible!

"But similarly, if it is at a given point, it must stay there, and will expend every erg staying there. It is then immovable! It is either irresistible in motion, or immovable in static condition. It is the irresistible and the immovable!

"What happens if the irresistible meets the immovable? It can only fight with its energy of existence, and the more energetic prevails."

CHAPTER X

IMPROVEMENTS AND CALCULATIONS

"It is still incredible. But you have done it. It is certainly successful!" said the Talsonian scientist with conviction.

Arcot shook his head. "Far from it — we have not realized a thousandth part of the tremendous possibilities of this invention. We must work and calculate and then invent.

"Think of the possibilities as a shield — naturally if we can make the matter we should be able to control its properties in any way we like. We should be able to make it opaque, transparent, or any color." Arcot was speaking to Morey now. "Do you remember, when we were caught in that cosmic ray field in space when we first left this universe, that I said that I had an idea for energy so vast that it would be impossible to describe its awful power?[1] I mentioned that I would attempt to liberate it if ever there was need? The need exists. I want to find that secret."

Stel Felso Theu was looking out through the window at a group of men excitedly beckoning. He called the attention of the others to them, and himself went out. Arcot and Wade joined him in a moment.

"They tell me that Fellsheh, well to the poleward of here has used four of its eight shots. They are still being attacked," explained the Talsonian gravely.

"Well, get in," snapped Arcot as he ran back to the ship. Stel Felso hastily followed, and the *Ancient Mariner* shot into the air, and darted away, poleward, to the Talsonian's directions. The ground fled behind them at a speed that made the scientist grip the hand-rail with a tenseness that showed his nervousness.

As they approached, a tremendous concussion and a great gout of light in the sky informed them of the early demise of several Thessians. But a real fleet was clustered about the city. Arcot approached low, and was able to get quite close before detection. His ray screen was up and Morey had charged the artificial matter apparatus, small as it was, for operation. He created a ball of substance outside the *Ancient Mariner*, and thrust it toward the nearest Thessian, just as a molecular hit the *Ancient Mariner*'s ray

---

1   *Islands of Space.*

screen.

The artificial matter instantly exploded with terrific violence, slightly denting the tremendously strong lux metal walls. The pressure of the light was so great that the inner relux walls were dented inward. The ground below was suddenly, instantaneously fused.

"Lord — they won't pass a ray screen, obviously," Morey muttered, picking himself from where he had fallen.

"Hey — easy there. You blinked off the ray screen, and our relux is seriously weakened," called Arcot, a note of worry in his voice.

"No artificial matter with the ray screen up. I'll use the magnet," called Morey.

He quickly shut off the apparatus, and went to the huge magnet control. The power room was crowded, and now that the battle was raging in truth, with three ships attacking simultaneously, even the enormous power capacity of the ship's generators was not sufficient, and the storage coils had been thrown into the operation. Morey looked at the instruments a moment. They were all up to capacity, save the ammeter from the coils. That wasn't registering yet. Suddenly it flicked, and the other instrument dropped to zero. They were in artificial space.

"Come here, will you, Morey," called Arcot. In a moment Morey joined his much worried friend.

"That artificial matter control won't work through ray screens. The Thessians never had to protect against moleculars here, and didn't have them up — hence the destruction wrought. We can't take our screen down, and we can't use our most deadly weapon with it up. If we had a big outfit, we might throw a screen around the whole ship, and sail right in. But we haven't."

"We can't stand ten seconds against that fleet. I'm going to find their base, and make them yell for help." Arcot snapped a tiny switch one notch further for the barest instant, then snapped it back. They were several millions miles from the planet. "Quicker," he explained, "to simply follow those ships back home — go back in time."

With the telectroscope, he took views at various distances, thus quickly tracing them back to their base at the pole of the planet. Instantly Arcot shot down, reaching the pole in less than a second, by carefully maneuvering of the space device.

A gigantic dome of polished relux rose from rocky, icy plains. The thing was nearly half a mile high, a mighty rounded roof that covered an area almost three-quarters of a mile in diameter.

Titanic — that was the only word that described it. About it there was the peculiar shimmer of a molecular ray screen.

Morey darted to the power room and set his apparatus into operation. He created a ball of matter outside the ship and hurled it instantly at the fort. It exploded with a terrific concussion as it hit the wall of the ray screen. Almost instantly a second one followed. The concussion was terrifically violent, the ground about was fused, and the ray screen was opened for a moment. Arcot threw all his moleculars on the screen, as Morey sent bomb after bomb at it. The coils supplied the energy, cracked the rock beneath. Each energy release disrupted the ray-screen for a moment, and the concentrated fury of the molecular beams poured through the opened screen, and struck the relux behind. It glowed opalescent now in a spot twenty feet across. But the relux was tremendously thick. Thirty bombs Morey hurled, while they held their position without difficulty, pouring their bombs and rays at the fort.

Arcot threw the ship into space, moved, and reappeared suddenly nearly three hundred yards further on. A snap of the eyes, and he saw that the fleet was approaching now. He went again into space, and retreated. Discretion was the better part of valor. But his plan had worked.

He waited half an hour, and returned. From a distance the telectroscope told him that one lone ship was patrolling outside the fort. He moved toward it, creeping up behind the icy mountains. His magnetic beam reached out. The ship lurched and fell. The magnetic beam reached out toward the fort, from which a molecular ray had flashed already, tearing up the icy waste which had concealed him. The ray-screen stopped it, while again Morey turned the magnetic beam on — this time against the fort. The ray remained on! Arcot retreated hastily.

"They found the secret, all right. No use, Morey, come on up," called the pilot. "They evidently put magnetic shielding around the apparatus. That means the magnetic beam is no good to us any more. They will certainly warn every other base, and have them install similar protection."

"Why didn't you try the magnetic ray on our first attack?" asked Zezdon Afthen.

"If it had worked, their sending apparatus would have been destroyed, and no message could have been sent to call their attackers off Fellsheh. By forcing them to recall their fleet I got results I couldn't get by attacking the fleet," Arcot said.

"I think there is little more I can do here, Stel Felso Theu. I will take you to Shesto, and there make final arrangements till my return, with apparatus capable of overthrowing your enemies. If you wish to accompany me — you may." He glanced around at the others of his party. "And our next move will be to return to Earth with what we have. Then we will investigate the Sirian planets, and learn anything they may have of interest, thence — to the real outer space, the utter void of intergalactic space, and an attempt to learn the secret of that enormous power."

They returned to Shesto, and there Arcot arranged that the only generator they could spare, the one already in their possession, might be used till other terrestrial ships could bring more. They left for Earth. Hour after hour they fled through the void, till at last old Sol was growing swiftly ahead of them, and finally Earth itself was large on the screens. They changed to a straight molecular drive, and dropped to the Vermont field from which they had taken off.

During the long voyage, Morey and Arcot had both spent much of the time working on the time-distortion field, which would give them a tremendous control over time, either speeding or slowing their time rate enormously. At last, this finished, they had worked on the artificial matter theory, to the point where they could control the shape of the matter perfectly, though as yet they could not control its exact nature. The possibility of such control was, however, definitely proven by the results the machines had given them. Arcot had been more immediately interested in the control of form. He could control the nature as to opacity or transparency to all vibrations that normal matter is opaque or transparent to. Light would pass, or not as he chose, but cosmics he could not stop nor would radio or moleculars be stopped by any present shield he could make.

They had signaled, as soon as they slowed outside the atmosphere, and when they settled to the field, Arcot's father and a number of very important scientists had already arrived.

Arcot senior greeted his son very warmly, but he was tremendously worried, as his son soon saw.

"What's happened, Dad — won't they believe your statements?"

"They doubted when I went to Luna for a session with the Interplanetary Council, but before they could say much, they had plenty of proof of my statements," the older man answered. "News came that a fleet of Planetary Guard ships had been wiped out by a fleet of ships from outer space. They were huge things — nearly half a mile in length. The Guard ships went up to them —

fifty of them — and tried to signal for a conference. The white ship was instantly wiped out — we don't know how. They didn't have ray screens, but that wasn't it. Whatever it was — slightly luminous ray in space — it simply released the energy of the lux metal and relux of the ship. Being composed of light energy simply bound by photonic attraction, it let go with terrible energy. They can do it almost instantly from a distance. The other Guards at once let loose with all their moleculars and cosmics. The enemy shunted off the moleculars, and wiped out the Guard almost instantly.

"Of course, I could explain the screen, but not the detonation ray. I am inclined to believe from other casualties that the destruction, though reported as an instantaneous explosion, was not that. Other ships have been destroyed, and they seemed to catch fire, and burn, but with terrific speed, more like gun powder than coal. It seems to start a spreading decomposition, the ship lasts perhaps ten minutes. If it went instantly, the shock of such a tremendous energy release would disrupt the planet.

"At any rate, the great fleet separated, twelve went to the North Pole of Earth, twelve to the south, and similarly twelve to each pole of Venus. Then one of them turned, and went back to wherever it had come from, to report. Just turned and vanished. Similarly one from Venus turned and vanished. That leaves twelve at each of the four poles, for, as I said, there were an even fifty.

"They all followed the same tactics on landing, so I'll simply tell what happened in Attica. In the North they had to pick one of the islands a bit to the south of the pole. They melted about a hundred square miles of ice to find one.

"The ships arranged themselves in a circle around the place, and literally hundreds of men poured out of each and fell to work. In a short time, they had set up a number of machines, the parts coming from the ships. These machines at once set to work, and they built up a relux wall. That wall was at least six feet thick; the floor was lined with thick relux as well as the roof, which is simply a continuation of the wall in a perfect dome. They had so many machines working on it, that within twenty-four hours they had it finished.

"We attacked twice, once in practically our entire force, with some ray-shield machines. The result was disastrous. The second attack was made with ray shielded machines only, and little damage was done to either side, though the enemy were somewhat impeded by masses of ice hurled into their position. Their relux disintegration ray was conspicuous by its absence.

"Yesterday — and it seems a lot longer than that, son — they started it again. They'd been unloading it from the ship evidently. We had had ray-shielded machines out, but they simply melted. They went down, and Earth retreated. They're in their fortress now. We don't know how to fight them. Now, for God's sake, tell us you have learned of some weapon, son!"

The older man's face was lined. His iron gray head showed his fatigue due to hours of concentration on his work.

"Some," replied Arcot briefly. He glanced around. Other men had arrived, men whom he met in his work. But there were Venerians here, too, in their protective suits, insulated against the cold of Earth, and against its atmosphere.

"First, though, gentlemen, allow me to introduce Stel Felso Theu of the planet Talso, one of our allies in this struggle, and Zezdon Afthen and Fentes of Ortol, one of our other allies.

"As to progress, I can say only that it is in a more or less rudimentary stage. We have the basis for great progress, a weapon of inestimable value — but it is only the basis. It must be worked out. I am leaving with you today the completed calculations and equations of the time field, the system used by the Thessian invaders in propelling their ships at a speed greater than that of light. Also, the uncompleted calculations in regard to another matter, a weapon which our ally, Talso, has given us, in exchange for the aid we gave in allowing them the use of one of our generators. Unfortunately the ship could not spare more than the single generator. I strongly advise rushing a number of generators to Talso in intergalactic freighters. They badly need power — power of respectable dimensions.

"I have stopped on Earth only temporarily, and I want to leave as soon as possible. I intend, however, to attempt an attack on the Arctic base of the Thessians, in strong hopes that they have not armored against one weapon that the *Ancient Mariner* carries — though I sadly fear that old Earth herself has played us false here. I hope to use the magnetic beam, but Earth's polar magnetism may have forced them to armor, and they may have sufficiently heavy material to block the effects."

Morey already had a ground crew servicing the ship. He gave designs to machinists on hand to make special control panels for the large artificial matter machines. Arcot and Wade got some badly needed equipment.

In six hours, Arcot had announced himself ready, and a squadron of Planetary Guard ships were ready to accompany the refitted *Ancient Mariner*.

They approached the pole cautiously, and were rewarded by the hiss and roar of ice melting into water which burst into steam under a ray. It was coming from an outpost of the camp, a tiny dome under a great mass of ice. But the dome was of relux. A molecular reached down from a Guard ship — and the Guard ship crumbled suddenly as dozens of moleculars from the points hit it.

"They know how to fight this kind of a war. That's their biggest advantage," muttered Arcot. Wade merely swore.

"Ray screens, no moleculars!" snapped Arcot into the transmitter. He was not their leader, but they saw his wisdom, and the squadron commander repeated the advice as an order. In the meantime, another ship had fallen. The dome had its screen up, allowing the multitudes of hidden stations outside to fight for it.

"Hmm — something to remember when terrestrians have to retire to forts. They will, too, before this war is over. That way the main fort doesn't have to lower its ray screen to fight," commented Arcot. He was watching intensely as a tiny ship swung away from one of the larger machines, and a tremendously powerful molecular started biting at the fort's ray screen. The ship seemed nothing but a flying ray projector, which was what it was.

As they had hoped, the deadly new ray stabbed out from somewhere on the side of the fort. It was not within the fort.

"Which means," pointed out Morey, "that they can't make stuff to stand that. Probably the projector would be vulnerable."

But a barrage of heat rays which immediately followed had no apparent effect. The little radio-controlled molecular beam projector lay on the rock under the melted ice, blazing incandescent with the rapidly released energy of the relux.

"Now to try the real test we came here for," Morey clambered back to the power room, and turned on the controls of the magnetic beam. The ship was aligned, and then he threw the last switch. The great mass of the machine jerked violently, and plunged forward as the beam attracted the magnetic core of the Earth.

Morey could not see it, but almost instantly the shimmer of the molecular screen on the fort died out. The deadly ray sprang out from the Thessian projector — and went dead. Frantically the Thessians tried weapon after weapon, and found them dead almost as soon as they were turned on — which was the natural result in the terrific magnetic field.

And these men had iron bones, their very bones were attracted by the beam; they plunged upward toward the ship as the beam touched them, but, accustomed to the enormous gravitation accelerations of an enormous world, most of them were not killed.

"Ah — !" exclaimed Arcot. He picked up the transmitter and spoke again to the Squadron Commander. "Squadron Commander Tharnton, what relux thickness does your ship carry?"

"Inch and a quarter," replied the surprised voice of the commander.

"Any of the other ships carry heavier?"

"Yes, the special solar investigator carries five inches. What shall we do?"

"Tell him to lower his screen, and let loose at once on all operating forts. His relux will stand for the time needed to shut them down for their own screens, unless some genius decides to fight it out. As soon as the other ships can lower their screens, tell them to do so, and tell them to join in. I'll be able to help then. My relux has been burned, and I'm afraid to lower the screen. It's mighty thin already."

The squadron commander was smiling joyously as he relayed the advice as a command.

Almost at once a single ship, blunt, an almost perfect cylinder, lowered its screen. In an instant the opalescence of the transformation showed on it, but its dozen ray projectors were at work. Fort after fort glowed opalescent, then flashed into protective ionization of screening. Quickly other ships lowered their screens, and joined in. In a moment more, the forts had been forced to raise their screens for protection.

A disc of artificial matter ten feet across suddenly appeared beside the *Ancient Mariner*. It advanced with terrific speed, struck the great dome of the fort, and the dome caved, bent in, bent still more — but would not puncture. The disc retreated, became a sharp cone, and drove in again. This time the point smashed through the relux, and made a small hole. The cone seemed to change gradually, melting into a cylinder of twenty foot diameter, and the hole simply expanded. It continued to expand as the cylinder became a huge disc, a hundred feet across, set in the wall.

Suddenly it simply dissolved. There was a terrific roar, and a mighty column of white rushed out of the gaping hole. Figures of Thessians caught by the terrific current came rocketing out. The inside was at last visible. The terrific pressure was hurling the outside line of ships about like thistledown. The *Ancient Mariner* reeled back under the tremendous blast of expanding gas. The snow that fell to the boiling water below was not water, *in toto*; some was carbon dioxide — and some oxygen chilled in the expansion of the gas. It was snowing within the dome. The falling forms of Thessians were robbed of the life-giving air pressure to which they were accustomed. But all this was visible for but an instant.

Then a small, thin sheet of artificial matter formed beside the fort, and advanced on the dome. Like a knife cutting open an orange, it simply went around the dome's edge, the great dome lifted like the lid of a teapot under the enormous gas pressure remaining — then dropped under its own weight.

The artificial matter was again a huge disc. It settled over the exact center of the dome — and went down. The dome caved in. It was crushed under a load utterly inestimable. Then the great disc, like some monstrous tamper, tamped the entire works of the Thessians into the bed-rock of the island. Every ship, every miniature fort, every man was caught under it — and annihilated.

The disc dissolved. A terrific barrage of heat beams played over the island, and the rock melted, flowed over the ruins, and left only the spumes of steam from the Arctic ice rising from a red-hot: mass of rock, contained a boiling pool.

The Battle of the Arctic was done.

CHAPTER XI

"WRITE OFF THE MAGNET"

"Squadron commander Tharnton speaking: Squadron 73-B of Planetary Guard will follow orders from Dr. Arcot directly. Heading south to Antarctica at maximum speed," droned the communicator. Under the official tone of command was a note of suppressed rage and determination. "And the squadron commander wishes Dr. Arcot every success in wiping out Antarctica as thoroughly and completely as he destroyed the Arctic base."

The flight of ships headed south at a speed that heated them white in the air, thin as it was at the hundred mile altitude, yet going higher would have taken unnecessary time, and the white heat meant no discomfort. They reached Antarctica in about ten minutes. The Thessian ships were just entering through great locks in the walls of the dome. At first sight of the terrestrial ships they turned, and shot toward the guard-ships. Their screens were down, for, armored as they were with very heavy relux they expected to be able to overcome the terrestrial thin relux before theirs was seriously impaired.

"Ships will put up screens." Arcot spoke sharply — a new plan had occurred to him. The moleculars of the Thessians Struck glowing screens, and no damage was done. "Ships, in order of number, will lower screen for thirty seconds, and concentrate all moleculars on one ship — the leader. Solar investigator will not join in action."

The flagship of the squadron lowered its screen, and a tremendous bombardment of rays struck the leading ship practically in one point. The relux glowed, and the opalescence shifted with bewildering, confusing colors. Then the terrestrial ship's screen was up, before the Thessians could concentrate on the one unprotected ship. Immediately another terrestrial ship opened its screen and bombarded the same ship. Two others followed — and then it was forced to use its screen.

But suddenly a terrestrial ship crashed. Its straining screen had been overworked — and it failed.

Arcot's magnetic beam went into action. The Thessian ray did not go out — it flickered, dimmed, but was apparently as deadly as ever.

"Shielded — write off the magnet, Morey. That is one asset we lose."

Arcot, protected in space, was thinking swiftly. Moleculars — useless. They had to keep their own screens up. Artificial matter — bound in by their own molecular screen! And the magnet had failed them against the protected mechanism of the dome. The ships were not as yet protected, but the dome was.

"Guess the only place we'd be safe is under the ground — way under!" commented Wade dryly.

"Under the ground — Wade, you're a genius!" Arcot gave a shout of joy, and told Wade to take over the ship.

"Take the ship back into normal space, head for the hill over behind the Dome, and drop behind it. It's solid rock, and even their rays will take a moment or so to move it. As soon as you get there, drop to the ground, and turn off the screen. No — here, I'll do it. You just take it there, land on the ground, and shut off the screen. I promise the rest!" Arcot dived for the artificial matter room.

The ship was suddenly in normal space; its screen up. The dog-fight had been ended. The terrestrial ships had been completely defeated. The *Ancient Mariner*'s appearance was a signal for all the moleculars in sight. Ten huge ships, half a dozen small forts and now the unshielded Dome, joined in. Their screen tubes heated up violently in the brief moment it took to dive behind the hill, a tube fused, and blew out. Automatic devices shunted it, another tube took the load — and heated. But their screen was full of holes before they were safe for the moment behind the hill.

Instantly Wade dropped the defective screen. Almost as quickly as the screen vanished, a cylinder of artificial matter surrounded the entire ship. The cylinder was tipped by a perfect cone of the same base diameter. The entire system settled into the solid rock. The rock above cracked and filled in behind them. The ship was suddenly pushed by the base of the cylinder behind them, and drove on through the rock, the cone parting the hard granite ahead. They went perhaps half a mile, then stopped. In the light of the ship's windows, they could see the faint mistiness of the inconceivably hard, artificial matter, and beyond the slick, polished surface of the rock it was pushing aside. The cone shape was still there.

There was a terrific roar behind them, the rock above cracked, shifted and moved about.

"Raying the spot where we went down," Arcot grinned happily.

The cone and cylinder merged, shifted together, and became a sphere. The sphere elongated upward and the *Ancient Mariner* turned in it, till it, too, pointed upward. The sphere became an ellipsoid.

Suddenly the ship was moving, accelerating terrifically. It plowed through the solid rock, and up — into a burst of light. They were *inside* the dome. Great ships were berthed about the floor. Huge machines bulked here and there — barracks for men — everything.

The ellipsoid shrank to a sphere, the sphere grew a protuberance which separated and became a single bar-like cylinder. The cylinder turned, and drove through the great dome wall. A little hole but it whirled rapidly around, sliced the top off neatly and quickly. Again, like a gigantic teapot lid, the whole great structure lifted, settled, and stayed there. Men, scrambling wildly toward ships, suddenly stopped, seemed to blur and their features ran together horribly. They fell — and were dead in an instant as the air disappeared. In another instant they were solid blocks of ice, for the temperature was below the freezing point of carbon dioxide.

The giant tamper set to work. The Thessian ships went first. They were all crumpled, battered wrecks in a few seconds of work of the terrible disc.

The dome was destroyed. Arcot tried something else. He put on his control machine the equation of a hyperboloid of two branches, and changed the constants gradually till the two branches came close. Then he forced them against each other. Instantly they fought, fought terribly for existence. A tremendous blast of light and heat exploded into being. The energy of two tons of lead attempted to maintain those two branches. It was not, fortunately, explosive, and it took place over a relux floor. Most of the energy escaped into space. The vast flood of light was visible on Venus, despite the clouds.

But it fused most of Antarctica. It destroyed the last traces of the camp in Antarctica.

"Well — the Squadron was wiped out, I see." Arcot's voice was flat as he spoke. The Squadron: twenty ships — four hundred men.

"Yes — but so is the Arctic camp, and the Antarctic camp, as well," replied Wade.

"What next, Arcot. Shall we go out to intergalactic space at once?" asked Morey, coming up from the power room.

"No, we'll go back to Vermont, and have the time-field stuff I ordered installed, then go to Sirius, and see what they have. They moved their planets from the gravitation field of Negra, their dead, black star, to the field of Sirius — and I'd like to know how they did it.[2] Then — Intergalactia." He started the ship toward Vermont, while Morey got into communication with the field, and gave them a brief report.

2 *The Black Star Passes.*

CHAPTER XII

SIRIUS

They landed about half an hour later, and Arcot simply went into the cottage, and slept — with the aid of a light soporific. Morey and Wade directed the disposition of the machines, but Dr. Arcot senior really finished the job. The machines would be installed in less than ten hours, for the complete plans Arcot and Morey had made, with the modern machines for translating plans to metal and lux had made the actual construction quick, while the large crew of men employed required but little time.

When Arcot and his friends awoke, the machines were ready.

"Well, Dad, you have the plans for all the machines we have. I expect to be back in two weeks. In the meantime you might set up a number of ships with very heavy relux walls, walls that will stand rays for a while, and equip them with the rudimentary artificial matter machines you have, and go ahead with the work on the calculations. Thett will land other machines here — or on the moon. Probably they will attempt to ray the whole Earth. They won't have concentration of ray enough to move the planet, or to seriously chill it. But life is a different matter — it's sensitive. It is quite apt to let go even under a mild ray. I think that a few exceedingly powerful ray screen stations might be set up, and the Heavyside Layer used to transmit the vibrations entirely around the Earth. You can see the idea easily enough. If you think it worthwhile — or better, if you can convince the thickheaded politicians of the Interplanatary Defense Commission that it is —

"Beyond that, I'll see you in about two weeks," Arcot turned, and entered the ship.

"I'll line up for Sirius and let go." Arcot turned the ship now, for Earth was well behind, and lined it on Sirius, bright in the utter black of space. He pushed his control to "1/2," and the space closed in about them. Arcot held it there while the chronometer moved through six and a half seconds. Sirius was at a distance almost planetary in its magnitude from them. Controlling directly now, he brought the ship closer, till a planet loomed large before them — a large world, its rocky continents, its rolling oceans and jagged valleys white under the enormous energy-flood from the gigantic star of Sirius, twenty-six times more brilliant than the sun they had left.

"But, Arcot, hadn't you better take it easy?" Wade asked.

"They might take us for enemies — which wouldn't be so good."

"I suppose it would be wise to go slowly. I had planned, as a matter of fact, on looking up a Thessian ship, taking a chance on a fight, and proving our friendship," replied Arcot.

Morey saw Arcot's logic — then suddenly burst into laughter. "Absolutely — attack a Thessian. But since we don't see any around now, we'll have to make one!"

Wade was completely mystified, and gave Morey a doubtful, sarcastic look. "Sounds like a good idea, only I wonder if this constant terrific mental strain —"

"Come along and find out!" Arcot threw the ship into artificial space for safety, holding it motionless. The planet, invisible to them, retreated from their motionless ship.

In the artificial matter control room, Arcot set to work, and developed a very considerable string of forms on his board, the equations of their formations requiring all the available formation controls.

"Now," said Arcot at last, "you stay here, Morey, and when I give the signal, create the thing back of the nearest range of hills, raise it, and send it toward us."

At once they returned to normal space, and darted down toward the now distant planet. They landed again near another city, one which was situated close to a range of mountains ideally suited to their purposes. They settled, while Zezdon Afthen sent out the message of friendship. He finally succeeded in getting some reaction, a sensation of scepticism, of distrust — but of interest. They needed friends, and only hoped that these were friends. Arcot pushed a little signal button, and Morey began his share of the play. From behind a low hill a slim, pointed form emerged, a beautifully streamlined ship, the lines obviously those of a Thessian, the windows streaming light, while the visible ionization about the hull proclaimed its molecular ray screen. Instantly Zezdon Afthen, who had carefully refrained from learning the full nature of their plans, felt the intense emotion of the discovery, called out to the others, while his thoughts were flashed to the Sirians below.

From the attacking ship, a body shot with tremendous speed, it flashed by, barely missing the *Ancient Mariner*, and buried itself in the hillside beyond. With a terrific explosion it burst, throwing the soil about in a tremendous crater. The *Ancient Mariner* spun about, turned toward the other ship, and let loose a tremendous bombardment of molecular and cosmic rays. A great flame of ionized air was the only result. A new ray reached out from the other ship, a fan-like spreading ray. It struck the *Ancient Mariner*, and did not harm it, though the hillside behind was suddenly withered and blackened, then smoking as the temperature rose.

Another projectile was launched from the attacking ship, and exploded terrifically but a few hundred feet from the *Ancient Mariner*. The terrestrial ship rocked and swayed, and even the distant attacker rocked under the explosion.

A projectile, glowing white, leaped from the Earthship. It darted toward the enemy ship, seemed to barely touch it, then burst into terrific flames that spread, eating the whole ship, spreading glowing flame. In an instant the blazing ship slumped, started to fall, then seemingly evaporated, and before it touched the ground, was completely gone.

The relief in Zezdon Afthen's mind was genuine, and it was easily obvious to the Sirians that the winning ship was friendly, for, with all its frightful armament, it had downed a ship obviously of Thett. Though not exactly like the others, it had the all too familiar lines.

"They welcome us now," said Zezdon Afthen's mental message to his companions.

"Tell them we'll be there — with bells on or thoughts to that effect," grinned Arcot. Morey had appeared in the doorway, smiling broadly.

"How was the show?" he asked.

"Terrible — Why didn't you let it fall, and break open?"

"What would happen to the wreckage as we moved?" he asked sarcastically. "I thought it was a darned good demonstration."

"It was convincing," laughed Arcot. "They want us now!"

The great ship circled down, landing gently just outside of the city. Almost at once one of the slim, long Sirian ships shot up from a courtyard of the city, racing out and toward the *Ancient Mariner*. Scarcely a moment later half a hundred other ships from all over the city were on the way. Sirians seemed quite humanly curious.

"We'll have to be careful here. We have to use altitude suits, as the Negrians breathe an atmosphere of hydrogen instead of oxygen," explained Arcot rapidly to the Ortolian and the Talsonian who were to accompany him. "We will all want to go, and so, although this suit will be decidedly uncomfortable for you and Zezdon Afthen and Stel Felso Theu, I think it wise that you all wear it. It will be much more convincing to the Sirians if we show that people of no less than three worlds are already interested in this alliance."

A considerable number of Sirian ships had landed about

them, and the tall, slim men of the 100,000,000-year-old race were watching them with their great brown eyes from a slight distance, for a cordon of men with evident authority were holding them back.

"Who are you, friends?" asked a single man who stood within the cordon. His strongly built frame, a great high brow and broad head designated him a leader at a glance.

Despite the vast change the light of Sirius had wrought, Arcot recognized in him the original photographs he had seen from the planet old Sol had captured as Negra had swept past. So it was he who answered the thought-question.

"I am of the third planet of the sun your people sought as a home a few years back in time, Taj Lamor. Because you did not understand us, and because we did not understand you, we fought. We found the records of your race on the planet our sun captured, and we know now what you most wanted. Had we been able to communicate with you then, as we can now, our people would never have fought.

"At last you have reached that sun you so needed, thanks, no doubt, to the genius that was with you.

"But now, in your new-found peace comes a new enemy, one who wants not only yours, but every sun in this galaxy.

"You have tried your ray of death, the anti-catalyst? And it but sputters harmlessly on their screens? You have been swept by their terrible rays that fuse mountains, then hurl them into space? Our world and the world of each of these men is similarly menaced.

"See, here is Zezdon Afthen, from Ortol, far on the other side of the galaxy, and here is Stel Felso Theu, of Talso. Their worlds, as well as yours and mine have been attacked by this menace from a distant galaxy, from Thett, of the sun Ansteck, of the galaxy Venone.

"Now we must form an alliance of far wider scope than ever has existed before.

"To you we have come, for your race is older by far than any race of our alliance. Your science has advanced far higher. What weapons have you discovered among those ancient documents, Taj Lamor? We have one weapon that you no doubt need; a screen, which will stop the rays of the molecule director apparatus. What have you to offer us?"

"We need your help badly," was the reply. "We have been able to keep them from landing on our planets, but it has cost us much. They have landed on a planet we brought with us when we left the black star, but it is not inhabited. From this as a base they have made attacks on us. We tried throwing the planet into Sirius. They merely left the planet hurriedly as it fell toward the star, and broke free from our attractive ray."

"The attractive ray! Then you have uncovered that secret?" asked Arcot eagerly.

Taj Lamor had some of his men bring an attractive ray projector to the ship. The apparatus turned out to be nearly a thousand tons in weight, and some twenty feet long, ten feet wide and approximately twelve feet high. It was impossible to load the huge machine into the *Ancient Mariner*, so an examination was conducted on the spot, with instruments whose reading was intelligible to the terrestrians operating it. Its principal fault lay in the fact that, despite the enormous energy of matter given out, the machine still gobbled up such titanic amounts of energy before the attraction could be established, that a very large machine was needed. The ray, so long as maintained, used no more power than was actually expended in moving the planet or other body. The power used while the ray was in action corresponded to the work done, but a tremendous power was needed to establish it, and this power could never be recovered.

Further, no reaction was produced in the machine, no matter what body it was turned upon. In swinging a planet then, a spaceship could be used as the base for the reaction was not exerted on the machine.

From such meager clues, and the instruments, Arcot got the hints that led him to the solution of the problem, for the documents, from which Taj Lamor had gotten his information, had been disastrously wiped out, when one of their cities fell, and Taj Lamor had but copied the machines of his ancestors.

The immense value of these machines was evident, for they would permit Arcot to do many things that would have been impossible without them. The explanation as he gave it to Stel Felso Theu, foretold the uses to which it might be put.

"As a weapon," he pointed out, "its most serious fault is that it takes a considerable time to pump in the power needed. It has here, practically the same fault which the artificial matter had on your world.

"As I see it, the ray is actually a directed gravitational field.

"Now here is one thing that makes it more interesting, and more useful. It seems to defy the laws of mechanics. It acts, but there is no apparent reaction! A small ship can swing a world! Remember, the field that generates the attraction is an integral, interwoven part of the mesh of Space. It is created by something outside of itself. Like the artificial matter, it exists there, and there alone. There is reaction on that attractive field, but it is created in Space at that given point, and the reaction is taken by all Space. No wonder it won't move.

"The work considerations are fairly obvious. The field is built up. That takes energy. The beam is focused on a body, the body falls nearer, and immediately absorbs the energy in acquiring a velocity. The machine replenishes the energy, because it is set to maintain a certain energy-level in the field. Therefore the machine must do the work of moving the ship, just as though it were a driving apparatus. After the beam has done what is wanted, it may be shut off, and the energy in the field is now available for any work needed. It may be drained back into power coils such as ours for instance, or one might just spend that last iota of power on the job.

"As a driving device it might be set to pull the entire ship along, and still not have any acceleration detectable to the occupants.

"I think we'll use that on our big ship," he finished, his eyes far away on some future idea.

"Natural gravity of natural matter is, luckily, not selective. It goes in all directions. But this artificial gravity is controlled so that it does not spread, and the result is that the mass-attraction of a mass of matter does not fall off as the inverse square of the distance, but like the ray from the parallel beam spotlight, continues undiminished.

"Actually, they create an exceedingly intense, exceedingly small gravitational field, and direct it in a straight line. The building up of this field is what takes time."

Zezdon Afthen, who had a question which was troubling him, looked anxiously at his friends. Finally he broke into their thoughts which had been too cryptically abbreviated for him to follow, like the work of a professor solving some problem, his steps taken so swiftly and so abbreviated that their following was impossible to his students.

"But how is it that the machine is not moved when exerting such force on some other body?" he asked at last.

"Oh, the ray concentrates the gravitational force, and projects it. The actual strain is in space. It is space that takes the strain, but in normal cases, unless the masses are very large, no considerable acceleration is produced over any great distance. That law operates in the case of the pulled body; it pulls the gravitational field as a normal field, the inverse-square law applying.

"But on the other hand, the gravity-beam pulls with a constant force.

"It might be likened to the light-pressure effects of a spotlight and a star. The spotlight would push the sun with a force that was constant; no matter what the distance, while the light pressure of the sun would vary as the inverse square of the distance.

"But remember, it is not a body that pulls another body, but a gravitational field that pulls another. The field is in space. A normal field is necessarily attached to the matter that it represents, or that represents it as you prefer, but this artificial field has no connection in the form of matter. It is a product of a machine, and exists only as a strain in space. To move it you must move all space, since it, like artificial matter, exists only where it is created in space.

"Do you see now why the law of action and reaction is apparently flouted? Actually the reaction is taken up by space."

Arcot rose, and stretched. Morey and Wade had been looking at him, and now they asked when he intended leaving for the intergalactic spaces.

"Now, I think. We have a lot of work to do. At present we have the mathematics of the artificial matter to carry on, and the math of the artificial gravity to develop. We gave the Sirians all we had on artificial matter and on moleculars.

"They gave us all they had — which wasn't much beyond the artificial gravity, and a lot of work. At any rate, let's go!"

CHAPTER XIII

ATTACKED

The *Ancient Mariner* stirred, and rose lightly from its place beside the city. Visible over the horizon now, and coming at terrific speed, was a fleet of seven Thessian ships.

They must do their best to protect that city. Arcot turned the ship and called his decision to Morey. As he did so, one of the Thessian ships suddenly swerved violently, and plunged downward. The attractive ray was in action. It struck the rocks of Neptune, and plunged in. Half buried, it stopped. Stopped — and backed out! The tremendously strong relux and lux had withstood the blow, and these strange, inhumanly powerful men had not been injured!

Two of the ships darted toward him simultaneously, flashing out molecular rays. The rays glanced off of Arcot's screen already in place, but the tubes were showing almost at once that this could not be sustained. It was evident that the swiftly approaching ships would soon break down the shields. Arcot turned the ship and drove to one side. His eyes went dead.

He cut into artificial space, waited ten seconds, then cut back. The scene before him changed. It seemed a different world. The light was very dim, so dim he could scarcely see the images on the view plate. They were so deep a red that they were very near to black. Even Sirius, the flaming blue-white star was red. The darting Thessian ships were moving quite slowly now, moving at a speed that was easy to follow. Their rays, before ionizing the air brilliantly red, were now dark. The instruments showed that the screen was no longer encountering serious loading, and, further, the load was coming in at a frequency harmlessly far down the radio spectrum!

Arcot stared in wide-eyed amazement. What could the Thessians have done that caused this change? He reached up and increased the amplification on the eyes to a point that made even the dim illumination sufficient. Wade was staring in amazement, too.

"Lord! What an idea!" suddenly exclaimed Arcot.

Wade was staring at Arcot in equally great amazement. "What's the secret?" he asked.

"Time, man, time! We are in an advanced time plane, living faster than they, our atoms of fuel are destroyed faster, our second is shorter. In one second of our earthly time our generators do the same amount of work as usual, but they do many, many times more work in one second, of the time we were in! We are under the advanced time field."

Wade could see it all. The red light — normal light seen through eyes enormously speeded in all perceptions. The change, the dimness — dim because less energy reached them per second of their time. Then came this blue light, as they reached the X-ray spectrum of Sirius, and saw X-rays as normal light — shielded, tremendously shielded by the atmosphere, but the enormous amplification of the eyes made up for it.

The remaining Thessians seemed to get the idea simultaneously, and started for Arcot in his own time field. The Thessian ship appeared to be actually leaping at him. Suddenly, his speed increased inconceivably. Simultaneously, Arcot's hand, already started toward the space-control switch, reached it, and pushed it to the point that threw the ship into artificial Space. The last glimmer of light died suddenly, as the Thessian ship's bow loomed huge beside the *Ancient Mariner.*

There was a terrific shock that hurled the ship violently to one side, threw the men about inside the ship. Simultaneously the lights blinked out.

Light returned as the automatic emergency incandescent lights in the room, fed from an energy store coil, flashed on abruptly. The men were white-faced, tense in their positions. Swiftly Morey was looking over the indicators on his remote-reading panel, while Arcot stared at the few dials before the actual control board.

"There's an air pressure outside the ship!" he cried out in surprise. "High oxygen, very little nitrogen, breathable apparently, provided there are no poisons. Temperature ten below zero C."

"Lights are off because relays opened when the crash short circuited them." Morey and the entire group were suddenly shaking.

"Nervous shock," commented Zezdon Afthen. "It will be an hour or more before we will be in condition to work."

"Can't wait," replied Arcot testily, his nerves on edge, too.

"Morey, make some good strong coffee if you can, and we'll waste a little air on some smokes."

Morey rose and went to the door that led through the main passage to the galley. "Heck of a job — no weight at all," he muttered. "There is air in the passage, anyway." He opened the door, and the air rushed from the control room to the passage till the pressure was equalized. The door to the power room was shut, but it was bulged, despite its two-inch lux metal, and through its clear material he could see the wreckage of the power room.

"Arcot," he called. "Come here and look at the power room. Quintillions of miles from home, we can't shut off this field now."

Arcot was with him in a moment. The tremendous mass of the nose of the Thessian ship had caught them full amid-ship, and the powerful ram had driven through the room. Their lux walls had not been touched; only a sledge-hammer blow would have bent them under any circumstances, let alone breaking them. But the tremendously powerful main generator was split wide open. And the mechanical damage was awful. The prow of the ship had been driven deep into the machine, and the power room was a wreck.

"And," pointed out Morey, "we can't handle a job like that. It will take a tremendous amount of machinery back on a planet to work that stuff, and we couldn't bend that bar, let alone fix it."

"Get the coffee, will you please, Morey? I have an idea that's bound to work," said Arcot looking fixedly at the machinery.

Morey turned and went to the galley.

Five minutes later they returned to the corridor, where Arcot stood still, looking fixedly at the engine room. They were carrying small plastic balloons with coffee in them.

They drank the coffee and returned to the control room, and sat about, the terrestrians smoking peacefully, the Ortolian and the Talsonian satisfying themselves with some form of mild narcotic from Ortol, which Zezdon Afthen introduced.

"Well, we have a lot more to do," Arcot said. "The air-apparatus stopped working a while back, and I don't want to sit around doing nothing while the air in the storage tanks is used up. Did you notice our friends, the enemy?" Through the great pilot's window the bulk of the Thessian ship's bow could be seen. It was cut across with an exactitude of mathematical certainty.

"Easy to guess what happened," Morey grinned. "They may have wrecked us, but we sure wrecked them. They got half in and half out of our space field. Result — the half that was in, stayed in. The half that was out stayed out. The two halves were instantaneously a billion miles apart, and that beautifully exact surface represents the point our space cut across.

"That being decided, the next question is how to fix this poor old wreck." Morey grinned a bit. "Better, how to get out of here, and down to old Neptune."

"Fix it!" replied Arcot. "Come on; you get in your space suit, take the portable telectroscope and set it up in space, motionless, in such a position that it views both our ship and the nose of the Thessian machine, will you, Wade? Tune it to — seven-seven-three." Morey rose with Arcot, and followed him, somewhat mystified, down the passage. At the airlock Wade put on his space suit, and the Ortolian helped him with it. In a moment the other three men appeared bearing the machine. It was practically weightless, though it would fall slowly if left to itself, for the mass of the *Ancient Mariner* and the front end of the Thessian ship made a considerable attractive field. But it was clumsy, and needed guiding here in the ship.

Wade took it into the airlock, and a moment later into space with him. His hand molecular-driving unit pulling him, he towed the machine into place, and with some difficulty got it practically motionless with respect of the two bodies, which were now lying against each other.

"Turn it a bit, Wade, so that the *Ancient Mariner* is just in its range," came Arcot's thoughts. Wade did so. "Come on back and watch the fun."

Wade returned. Arcot and the others were busy placing a heavy emergency lead from the storeroom in the place of one of the broken leads. In five minutes they had it fixed where they wanted it.

Into the control room went Arcot, and started the power-room teleview plate. Connected into the system of view plates, the scene was visible now on all the plates in the ship. Well off to one side of the room, prepared for such emergencies, and equipped with individual power storage coils that would run it for several days, the view plate functioned smoothly.

"Now, we are ready," said Arcot. The Talsonian proved he understood Arcot's intentions by preceding him to the laboratory.

Arcot had two viewplates operating here. One was covering the scene as shown by the machine outside, and the other showed the power room.

Arcot stepped over to the artificial-matter machine, and worked swiftly on it. In a moment the power from the storage coils of the ship was flowing through the new cable, and into the machine. A huge ring appeared about the nose of the Thessian ship, fitting snugly over it. A terrific wrench — and it was free of the *Ancient Mariner*. The ring contracted and formed a chunk of the stuff free of the broken nose of the ship.

It was carried over to the wall of the *Ancient Mariner*, a smaller piece snipped off as before, and carried inside. A piece of perhaps half a ton mass. "I hope they use good stuff," grinned Arcot. The piece was deposited on the floor of the ship, and a disc formed of artificial matter plugged the hole in its side. Another took a piece of the relux from the broken Thessian ship, pushed it into the hole on the ship. The space about the scene of operation was a crackling inferno of energy breaking down into heat and light. Arcot dematerialized his tremendous tools, and the wall of the *Ancient Mariner* was neatly patched with relux smoothed over as perfectly as before. A second time, using some of the relux he had brought within the ship, and the inner wall was rebuilt. The job was absolutely perfect, save that now, where there had been lux, there was an outer wall of relux.

The main generator was crumpled up, and torn out. The auxiliary generators would have to carry the load. The great cables were swiftly repaired in the same manner, a perfect cylinder forming about them, and a piece of relux from the store Arcot had sliced from the enemy ship, welding them perfectly under enormous pressure, pressure that made them flow perfectly into one another as heat alone could not.

In less than half an hour the ship was patched up, the power room generally repaired, save for a few minor things that had to be replaced from the stores. The main generator was gone, but that was not an essential. The door was straightened and the job done.

In an hour they were ready to proceed.

CHAPTER XIV

INTERGALACTIC SPACE

"Well, Sirius has retreated a bit," observed Arcot. The star was indeed several trillions of miles away. Evidently they had not been motionless as they had thought, but the interference of the Thessian ship had thrown their machine off.

"Shall we go back, or go on?" asked Morey.

"The ship works. Why return?" asked Wade. "I vote we go on."

"Seconded," added Arcot.

"If they who know most of the ship vote for a continuance of the journey, then assuredly we who know so little can only abide by their judgment. Let us continue," said Zezdon Afthen gravely.

Space was suddenly black about them. Sirius was gone, all the jewels of the heavens were gone in the black of swift flight. Ten seconds later Arcot lowered the space-control. Black behind them the night of space was pricked by points of light, the infinite multitude of the stars. Before them lay — nothing. The utter emptiness of space between the galaxies.

"Thlek Styrs! What happened?" asked Morey in amazement, his pet Venerian phrase rolling out in his astonishment.

"Tried an experiment, and it was overly successful," replied Arcot, a worried look on his face. "I tried combining the Thessian high speed *time* distortion with our high *speed* space distortion — both on low power. 'There ain't no sich animals,' as the old agriculturist remarked of the giraffe. God knows what speed we hit, but it was plenty. We must be ten thousand light years beyond the galaxy."

"That's a fine way to start the trip. You have the old star maps to get back however, have you not?" asked Wade.

"Yes, the maps we made on our first trip out this way are in the cabinet. Look 'em up, will you, and see how far we have to go before we reach the cosmic fields?"

Arcot was busy with his instruments, making a more accurate determination of their distance from the "edge" of the galaxy. He adopted the figure of twelve thousand five hundred light years as the probable best result. Wade was back in a moment with the information that the fields lay about sixteen thousand light years out. Arcot went on, at a rate that would reach the fields in two hours.

Several hours more were spent in measurements, till at last Arcot announced himself satisfied.

"Good enough — back we go." Again in the control room, he threw on the drive, and shot through the twenty-seven thousand light years of cosmic ray fields, and then more leisurely returned to the galaxy. The star maps were strangely off. They could follow them, but only with difficulty as the general configuration of the constellations that were their guides were visibly altered to the naked eye.

"Morey," said Arcot softly, looking at the constellation at which they were then aiming, and at the map before him, "there is something very, very rotten. The Universe either 'ain't what it used to be' or we have traveled in more than space."

"I know it, and I agree with you. Obviously, from the degree of alteration off the constellations, we are off by about 100,000 years. Question: how come? Question: what are we going to do about it?"

"Answer one: remembering what we observed *in re* Sirius, I suspect that the interference of that Thessian ship, with its time-field opposing our space-field did things to our time-frame. We were probably thrown off then.

"As to the second question, we have to determine number one first. Then we can plan our actions."

With Wade's help, and by coming to rest near several of the stars, then observing their actual motions, they were able to determine their time-status. The estimate they made finally was of the order of eighty thousand years in the past! The Thessian ship had thrown them that much out of their time.

"This isn't all to the bad," said Morey with a sigh. "We at least have all the time we could possibly use to determine the things we want for this fight. We might even do a lot of exploring for the archeologists of Earth and Venus and Ortol and Talso. As to getting back — that's a question."

"Which is," added Arcot, "easy to answer now, thank the good Lord. All we have to do is wait for our time to catch up with us. If we just wait eighty thousand years, eight hundred centuries, we will be in our own time."

"Oh, I think waiting so long would be boring," said Wade sarcastically. "What do you suggest we do in the intervening eighty millenniums? Play cards?"

"Oh, cards or chess. Something like that," grinned Arcot. "Play cards, calculate our fields — and turn on the time rate control."

"Oh — I take it back. You win! Take all! I forgot all about that," Wade smiled at his friend. "That will save a little waiting, won't it."

"The exploring of our worlds would without doubt be of infinite benefit to science, but I wonder if it would not be of more direct benefit if we were to get back to our own time, alive and well. Accidents always happen, and for all our weapons, we might easily meet some animal which would put an abrupt and tragic finish to our explorations. Is it not so?" asked Stel Felso Theu.

"Your point is good, Stel Felso Theu. I agree with you. We will do no more exploring than is necessary, or safe."

"We might just as well travel slowly on the time retarder, and work on the way. I think the thing to do is to go back to Earth, or better, the solar system, and follow the sun in its path."

They returned, and the desolation that the sun in its journey passes through is nothing to the utter, oppressive desolation of empty space between the stars, for it has its family of planets — and it has no conscious thought.

The Sun was far from the point that it had occupied when the travelers had left it, billions on billions of miles further on its journey around the gravitational center of our galactic universe, and in the eighty millenniums that they must wait, it would go far.

They did not go to the planets now, for, as Arcot said in reply to Stel Felso Theu's suggestion that they determine more accurately their position in time, life had not developed to an extent that would enable them to determine the year according to our calendar.

So for thirty thousand years they hung motionless as the sun moved on, and the little spots of light, that were worlds, hurled about it in a mad race. Even Pluto, in its three-hundred-year-long track seemed madly gyrating beneath them; Mercury was a line of light, as it swirled about the swiftly moving sun.

But that thirty thousand years was thirty days to the men of the ship. Their time rate immensely retarded, they worked on their calculations. At the end of that month Arcot had, with the help of Morey and Wade, worked out the last of the formulas of artificial matter, and the machines had turned out the last graphical function of the last branch of research that they could discover. It was a time of labor for them, and they worked almost constantly, stopping occasionally for a game of some sort to relax the nervous tension.

At the end of that month they decided that they would go to Earth.

They speeded their time rate now, and flashed toward Earth

at enormous speed that brought them within the atmosphere in minutes. They had landed in the valley of the Nile. Arcot had suggested this as a means of determining the advancement of life of man. Man had evidently established some of his earliest civilizations in this valley where water and sun for his food plants were assured.

"Look — there *are* men here!" exclaimed Wade. Indeed, below them were villages, of crude huts made of timber and stone and mud. Rubble work walls, for they needed little shelter here, and the people were but savages.

"Shall we land?" asked Arcot, his voice a bit unsteady with suppressed excitement.

"Of course!" replied Morey without turning from his station at the window. Below them now, less than half a mile down on the patchwork of the Nile valley, men were standing, staring up, collecting in little groups, gesticulating toward the strange thing that had materialized in the air above them.

"Does every one agree that we land?" asked Arcot.

There were no dissenting voices, and the ship sank gently toward a road below and to the left. A little knot of watchers broke, and they fled in terror as the great machine approached, crying out to their friends, casting affrighted glances at the huge, shining monster behind them.

Without a jar the mighty weight of the ship touched the soil of its native planet, touched it fifty millenniums before it was made, five hundred centuries before it left!

Arcot's brow furrowed. "There is one thing puzzles me — I can't see how we can come back. Don't you see, Morey, we have disturbed the lives of those people. We have affected history. This must be written into the history that exists.

"This seems to banish the idea of free thought. We have changed history, yet history is that which is already done!

"Had I never been born, had — but I *was* already — I existed fifty-eighty thousand years before I was born!"

"Let's go out and think about that later. We'll go to a psych hospital, if we don't stop thinking about problems of space and time for a little while. We need some kind of relaxation."

"I suggest that we take our weapons with us. These men may have weapons of chemical nature, such as poisons injected into the flesh on small sticks hurled either by a spring device or by pneumatic pressure of the lungs," said Stel Felso Theu as he rose from his seat unstrapping himself.

"Arrows and blow-guns we call 'em. But it's a good idea, Stel

Felso, and I think we will," replied Arcot. "Let's not all go out at once, and the first group to go out goes out on foot, so they won't be scared off by our flying around."

Arcot, Wade, Zezdon Afthen, and Stel Felso Theu went out. The natives had retreated to a respectful distance, and were now standing about, looking on, chattering to themselves. They were edging nearer.

"Growing bold," grinned Wade.

"It is the characteristic of intelligent races manifesting itself — curiosity," pointed out Stel Felso Theu.

"Are these the type of men still living in this valley, or who will be living there in fifty thousand years?" asked Zezdon Afthen.

"I'd say they weren't Egyptians as we know them, but typical Neolithic men. It seems they have brains fully as large as some of the men I see on the streets of New York. I wonder if they have the ability to learn as much as the average man of — say about 1950?"

The Neolithic men were warming up. There was an orator among them, and his grunts, growls, snorts and gestures were evidently affecting them. They had sent the women back (by the simple and direct process of sweeping them up in one arm and heaving them in the general direction of home). The men were brandishing polished stone knives and axes, various instruments of war and peace. One favorite seemed to be a large club.

"Let's forestall trouble," suggested Arcot. He drew his ray pistol, and turned it on the ground directly in front of them, and about halfway between them and the Neoliths. A streak of the soil about two feet wide flashed into intense radiation under the impact of millions on millions of horsepower of radiant energy. Further, it was fused to a depth of twenty feet or more, and intensely hot still deeper. The Neoliths took a single look at it, then turned, and raced for home.

"Didn't like our looks. Let's go back."

They wandered about the world, investigating various peoples, and proved to their own satisfaction that there was no Atlantis, not at this time at any rate. But they were interested in seeing that the polar caps extended much farther toward the equator; they had not retreated at that time to the extent that they had by the opening of history.

They secured some fresh game, an innovation in their larder, and a welcome one. Then the entire ship was swept out with fresh, clean air, their water tanks filled with water from the cold streams of the melting glaciers. The air apparatus was given a new stock to work over.

Their supplies in a large measure restored, thousands of aerial photographic maps made, they returned once more to space to wait.

Their time was taken up for the most part by actual work on the enormous mass of calculation necessary. It is inconceivable to the layman what tremendous labor is involved in the development of a single mathematical hypothesis, and a concrete illustration of it was the long time, with tremendously advanced calculating machines, that was required in their present work.

They had worked out the problem of the time-field, but there they had been aided by the actual apparatus, and the possibilities of making direct tests on machines already set up. The problem of artificial matter, at length fully solved, was a different matter. This had required within a few days of a month (by their clocks; close to thirty thousand years of Earth's time), for they had really been forced to develop it all from the beginning. In the small improvements Arcot had instituted in Stel Felso Theu's device, he had really merely followed the particular branch that Stel Felso Theu had stumbled upon. Hence it was impossible to determine with any great variety, the type of matter created. Now, however, Arcot could make any known kind of matter, and many unknown kinds.

But now came the greatest problem of all. They were ready to start work on the data they had collected in space.

"What," asked Zezdon Afthen, as he watched the three terrestrians begin their work, "is the nature of the thing you are attempting to harness?"

"In a word, energy," replied Arcot, pausing.

"We are attempting to harness energy in its primeval form, in the form of a space-field. Remember, mass is a measure of energy. Two centuries ago a scientist of our world proposed the idea that energy could be measured by mass, and proceeded to prove that the relationship was the now firmly intrenched formula $E=Mc^2$.

"The sun is giving off energy. It is giving off mass, then, in the form of light photons. The field of the sun's gravity must be constantly decreasing as its mass decreases. It is a collapsing field. It is true, the sun's gravitational field does decrease, by a minute amount, despite the fact that our sun loses a thousand million tons of matter every four minutes. The percentage change is minute, but the energy released is — immeasurable.

"But, I am going to invent a new power unit, Afthen. I will call it the 'sol,' the power of a sun. One sol is the rating of our sun. And I will measure the energy I use in terms of sun-powers, not horse-power. That may tell you of its magnitude!"

"But," Zezdon Afthen asked, "while you men of Earth work on this problem, what is there for us? We have no problems, save the problem of the fate of our world, still fifty thousand years of your time in the future. It is terrible to wait, wait, wait and think of what may be happening in that other time. Is there nothing we can do to help? I know our hopeless ignorance of your science. Stel Felso Theu can scarcely understand the thoughts you use, and I can scarcely understand his explanations! I cannot help you there, with your calculations, but is there nothing I can do?"

"There is, Ortolian, decidedly. We badly need your help, and as Stel Felso Theu cannot aid us here as much as he can by working with you, I will ask him to do so. I want your knowledge of psycho-mechanical devices to help us. Will you make a machine controlled by mental impulses? I want to see such a system and know how it is done that I may control machines by such a system."

"Gladly. It will take time, for I am not the expert worker that you are, and I must make many pieces of apparatus, but I will do what I can," exclaimed Zezdon Afthen eagerly.

So, while Arcot and his group continued their work of determining the constants of the space-energy field, the others were working on the mental control apparatus.

CHAPTER XV
ALL-POWERFUL GODS

Again there was a period of intense labor, while the ship drifted through time, following Earth in its mad careening about the sun, and the sun as it rushed headlong through space. At the end of a thirty-day period, they had reached no definite position in their calculations, and the Talsonian reported, as a medium between the two parties of scientists, that the work of the Ortolian had not reached a level that would make a scientific understanding possible.

As the ship needed no replenishing, they determined to finish their present work before landing, and it was nearly forty thousand years after their first arrival that they again landed on Earth.

It was changed now; the ice caps had retreated visibly, the Nile delta was far longer, far more prominent, and cities showed on the Earth here and there.

Greece, they decided would be the next stop, and to Greece they went, landing on a mountain side. Below was a village, a small village, a small thing of huts and hovels. But the villagers attacked, swarming up the hillside furiously, shouting and shrieking warnings of their terrible prowess to these men who came from the "shining house," ordering them to flee from them and turn over their possession to them.

"What'll we do?" asked Morey. He and Arcot had come out alone this time.

"Take one of these fellows back with us, and question him. We had best get a more or less definite idea of what time-age we are in, hadn't we? We don't want to overshoot by a few centuries, you know!"

The villagers were swarming up the side of the hill, armed with weapons of bronze and wood. The bronze implements of murder were rare, and evidently costly, for those that had them were obviously leaders, and better dressed than the others.

"Hang it all, I have only a molecular pistol. Can't use that, it would be a plain massacre!" exclaimed Arcot.

But suddenly several others, who had come up from one side, appeared from behind a rock. The scientists were wearing their power suits, and had them on at low power, leaving a weight of about fifty pounds. Morey, with his normal weight well over two hundred, jumped far to one side of a clumsy rush of a peasant, leaped back, and caught him from behind. Lifting the smaller man above his head, he hurled him at two others following. The three went down in a heap.

Most of the men were about five feet tall, and rather lightly built. The "Greek God" had not yet materialized among them. They were probably poorly fed, and heavily worked. Only the leaders appeared to be in good physical condition, and the men could not develop to large stature. Arcot and Morey were giants among them, and with their greater skill, tremendous jumping ability, and far greater strength, easily overcame the few who had come by the side. One of the leaders was picked up, and trussed quickly in a rope a fellow had carried.

"Look out," called Wade from above. Suddenly he was standing beside them, having flown down on the power suit. "Caught your thoughts — rather Zezdon Afthen did." He handed Arcot a ray pistol. The rest of the Greeks were near now, crying in amazement, and running more slowly. They didn't seem so anxious to attack. Arcot turned the ray pistol to one side.

"Wait!" called Morey. A face peered from around the rock toward which Arcot had aimed his pistol. It was that of a girl, about fifteen years old in appearance, but hard work had probably aged her face. Morey bent over, heaved on a small boulder, about two hundred pounds of rock, and rolled it free of the depression it rested in, then caught it on a molecular ray, hurled it up. Arcot turned his heat ray on it for an instant, and it was white hot. Then the molecular ray threw it over toward the great rock, and crushed it against it. Three children shrieked and ran out from the rock, scurrying down the hillside.

The soldiers had stopped. They looked at Morey. Then they looked at the great rock, three hundred yards from him. They looked at the rock fragments.

"They think you threw it," grinned Arcot.

"What else — they saw me pick it up, saw me roll it, and it flew. What else could they think?"

Arcot's heat ray hissed out, and the rocks sputtered and cracked, then glowed white. There was a dull explosion, and chips of rock flew up. Water, imprisoned, had been turned into steam. In a moment the whistle and crackle of combined heat and molecular rays stabbing out from Arcot's hands had built a barrier of fused rocks.

Leisurely Arcot and Morey carried their now revived prisoner back to the ship, while Wade flew ahead to open the locks.

Half an hour later the prisoner was discharged, much to his

surprise, and the ship rose. They had been able to learn nothing from him. Even the Greek Gods, Zeus, Hermes, Apollo, all the later Greek gods, were unknown, or so greatly changed that Arcot could not recognize them.

"Well," he said at length, "it seems all we know is that they came before any historical Greeks we know of. That puts them back quite a bit, but I don't know how far. Shall we go see the Egyptians?"

They tried Egypt, a few moments across the Mediterranean, landing close to the mouth of the Nile. The people of a village near by immediately set out after them. Better prepared this time, Arcot flew out to meet them with Zezdon Afthen and Stel Felso Theu. Surely, he felt, the sight of the strange men would be no more terrifying than the ship or the men flying. And that did not seem to deter their attack. Apparently the proverb that "Discretion is the better part of valor," had not been invented.

Arcot landed near the head of the column, and cut off two or three men from the rest with the aid of his ray pistol. Zezdon Afthen quickly searched his mind, and with Arcot's aid they determined he did not know any of the Gods that Arcot suggested.

Finally they had to return to the ship, disappointed. They had had the slight satisfaction of finding that the Sun God was Ralz, the later Egyptian Ra might well have been an evolved form of that name.

They restocked the ship, fresh game and fruits again appearing on the menu, then once again they launched forth into space to wait for their own time.

"It seems to me that we must have produced some effect by our visit," said Arcot, shaking his head solemnly.

"We did, Arcot," replied Morey softly. "We left an impress in history, an impress that still is, and an impress that affected countless thousands."

"Meet the Egyptian Gods with their heads strange to terrestrians, the Gods who fly through the air without wings, come from a shining house that flies, whose look, whose pointed finger melts the desert sands, and the moist soil!" he continued softly, nodding toward the Ortolian and the Talsonian.

"Their 'impossible' Gods existed, and visited them. Indubitably some genius saw that here was a chance for fame and fortune and sold 'charms' against the 'Gods.' Result: we are carrying with us some of the oldest deities. Again, we did leave our imprint in history."

"And," cried Wade excitedly, "meet the great Hercules, who

threw men about. I always knew that Morey was a brainless brute, but I never realized the marvelous divining powers of those Greeks so perfectly — now, the Incarnation of Dumb Power!" Dramatically Wade pointed to Morey, unable even now to refrain from some unnecessary comments.

"All right, Mercury, the messenger of the Gods speaks. The little flaps on Wade's flying shoes must indeed have looked like the winged shoes of legend. Wade was Mercury, too brainless for anything but carrying the words of wisdom uttered by others.

"And Arcot," continued Morey, releasing Wade from his condescending stare, "is Jove, hurling the rockfusing, destroying thunderbolts!"

"The Gods that my friends have been talking of," explained Arcot to the curious Ortolians, "are legendary deities of Earth. I can see now that we did leave an imprint on history in the only way we could — as Gods, for surely no other explanation could have occurred to those men."

The days passed swiftly in the ship, as their work approached completion. Finally, when the last of the equation of Time, artificial matter, and the most awful of their weapons, the unlimited Cosmic Power, had been calculated, they fell to the last stage of the work. The actual appliances were designed. Then the completed apparatus that the Ortolian and the Talsonian had been working on, was carefully investigated by the terrestrial physicists, and its mechanism studied. Arcot had great plans for this, and now it was incorporated in their control apparatus.

The one remaining problem was their exact location in time. Already their progress had brought them well up to the nineteenth century, but, as Morey sadly remarked, they couldn't tell what date, for they were sadly lacking in history. Had they known the real date, for instance, of the famous battle of Bull Run, they could have watched it in the telectroscope, and so determined their time. As it was, they knew only that it was one of the periods of the first half of the decade of 1860.

"As historians, we're a bunch of first-class kitchen mechanics. Looks like we're due for another landing to locate the exact date," agreed Arcot.

"Why land now? Let's wait until we are nearer the time to which we belong, so we won't have to watch so carefully and so long," suggested Wade.

They argued this question for about two hundred years as a matter of fact. After that, it was academic anyway.

CHAPTER XVI

HOME AGAIN

They were getting very near their own time, Arcot felt. Indeed, they must already exist on Earth. "One thing that puzzles me," he commented, "is what would happen if we were to go down now, and see ourselves."

"Either we can't or we don't want to do it," pointed out Morey, "because we didn't."

"I think the answer is that nothing can exist two times at the same time-rate," said Arcot. "As long as we were in a different time-rate we could exist at two times. When we tried to exist simultaneously, we could not, and we were forced to slip through time to a time wherein we either did not exist or wherein we had not yet been. Since we were nearer the time when we last existed in normal time, than we were to the time of our birth, we went to the time we left. I suspect that we will find we have just left Earth. Shall we investigate?"

"Absolutely, Arcot, and here's hoping we didn't overshoot the mark by much." As Morey intimated, had they gone much beyond the time they left Earth, they might find conditions very serious, indeed. But now they went at once toward Earth on the time control. As they neared, they looked anxiously for signs of the invasion. Arcot spotted the only evident signs, however; two large spheres, tiny points in appearance on the telectroscope screen, were circling Earth, one at about 1,000 miles, moving from east to west, the other about 1,200 miles moving from north to south.

"It seems the enemy have retreated to space to do their fighting. I wonder how long we were away."

As they swept down at a speed greater than light, they were invisible till Arcot slowed down near the atmosphere. Instantly half a dozen fast ships darted toward them, but the ship was very evidently unlike the Thessian ships, and no attack was made. First the occupants would have an opportunity to prove their friendliness.

"Terrestrians Arcot, Morey and Wade reporting back from exploration in space, with two friends. All have been on Earth with us previously," said Arcot into the radio vision apparatus.

"Very well, Dr. Arcot. You are going to New York or Vermont?" asked the Patrol commander.

"Vermont."

"Yes, Sir. I'll see that you aren't stopped again."

And, thanks to the message thus sent ahead, they were not, and in less than half an hour they landed once more in Vermont, on the field from which they had started.

The group of scientists who had been here on their last call had gone, which seemed natural enough to them, who had been working for three months in the interval of their trip, but to Dr. Arcot senior, as he saw them, it was a misfortune.

"Now I never will get straight all you'll have ready, and I didn't expect you back till next week. The men have all gone back to their laboratories, since that permits of better work on the part of each, but we can call them here in half an hour. I'm sure they'll want to come. What did you learn, Son, or haven't you done any calculating on your data as yet?"

"We learned plenty, and I feel quite sure that a hint of what we have would bring all those learning-hounds around us pretty quickly, Dad," laughed Arcot junior, "and believe it or not, we've been calculating on this stuff for three months since we left yesterday!"

"What!"

"Yes, it's true! We were on our time field, and turned on the space control — and a Thessian ship picked that moment to run into us. We cut the ship in half as neatly as you please, but it threw us eighty thousand years into the past. We have been coasting through time on retarded rate while Earth caught up with itself, so to speak. In the meantime — three months in a day!

"But don't call those men. Let them come to the appointment, while we do some work, and we have plenty of work to do, I assure you. We have a list of things to order from the standard supply houses, and I think you better get them for us, Dad." Arcot's manner became serious now. "We haven't gotten our Government Expense Research Cards yet, and you have. Order the stuff, and get it out here, while we get ready for it. Honestly, I believe that a few ships such as this apparatus will permit, will be enough in themselves to do the job. It really is a pity that the other men didn't have the opportunity we had for crowding much work into little time!

"But then, I wouldn't want to take that road to concentration again myself!

"Have the enemy amused you in my absence? Come on, let's sit down in the house instead of standing here in the sun."

They started toward the house, as Arcot senior explained what had happened in the short time they had been away.

"There is a friend of yours here, whom you haven't seen in some time, Son. He came with some allies."

As they entered the house, they could hear the boards creak under some heavy weight that moved across the floor, soundlessly and light of motion in itself. A shadow fell across the hall floor, and in the doorway a tremendously powerfully-built figure stood.

He seemed to overflow the doorway, nearly six and a half feet tall, and fully as wide as the door. His rugged, bronzed face was smiling pleasantly, and his deep-set eyes seemed to flash; a living force flowed from them.

"Torlos! By the Nine Planets! Torlos of Nansal! Say, I didn't expect you here, and I will not put my hand in that meatgrinder of yours," grinned Arcot happily, as Torlos stretched forth a friendly, but quite too powerful hand.

Torlos of Nansal, that planet Arcot had discovered on his first voyage across space, far in another Island of Space, another Island Universe, was not constructed as are human beings of Earth, nor of Venus, Talso, or Ortol, but most nearly resembled, save in size, the Thessians. Their framework, instead of being stone, as is ours, was iron, their bones were pure metallic iron, far stronger than bone. On these far stronger bones were great muscles of an entirely different sort, a muscle that used heat of the body as its fuel, a muscle that was utterly tireless, and unbelievably powerful. Not a chemical engine, but a molecular motion engine, it had no chemical fatigue-products that would tire it, and needed only the constant heat supply the body sucked from the air to work indefinitely. Unlimited by waste-carrying considerations, the strength was enormous.

It was one of the commercial space freighters plying between Nansal, Sator, Earth and Venus that had brought the news of this war to him, Torlos explained, and he, as the new Trade Coordinator and Fourth of the Four who now ruled Nansal, had suggested that they go to the aid of the man who had so aided them in their great war with Sator. It was Arcot's gift of the secret of the molecular ray and the molecular ship that had enabled them to overcome their enemy of centuries, and force upon them an unwelcome peace.

Now, with a fleet of fifty interstellar, or better, intergalactic battleships, Nansal was coming to Earth's aid.

The battleships were now on patrol with all of Earth's and Venus' fleet. But the Nansalian ships were all equipped with the enormously rapid space distortion system of travel, of course, and were a shock troop in the patrol. The Terrestrian and Venerian patrols were not so equipped in full.

"And Arcot, from what I have learned from your father, it seems that I can be of real assistance," finished Torlos.

"But now, I think, I should know what the enemy has done. I see they built some forts."

"Yes," replied Arcot senior, "they did. They decided that the system used on the forts of North and South poles was too effective. They moved to space, and cut off slices of Luna, pulled it over on their molecular rays, and used some of the most magnificent apparatus you ever dreamed of. I have just started working on the mathematics of it.

"We sent out a fleet to do some investigating, but they attacked, and stopped work in the meantime. Whatever the ray is that can destroy matter at a distance, they are afraid that we could find its secret too easily, and block it, for they don't think it is a weapon, and it is evidently slow in action."

"Then it isn't what I thought it was," muttered Arcot.

"What did you think it was?" asked his father.

"Er — tell you later. Go on with the account."

"Well, to continue. We have not been idle. Following your suggestion, we built up a large ray screen apparatus, in fact, several of them, and carried them in ships to different parts of the world. Also some of the planets, lest they start dropping worlds on us. They are already in operation, sending their defensive waves against the Heaviside layer. Radio is poor, over any distance, and we can't call Venus from inside the layer now. However, we tested the protection, and it works — far more efficiently than we calculated, due to the amazing conductivity of the layer.

"If they intend to attack in that way, I suspect that it will be soon, for they are ready now, as we discovered. An attack on their fort was met with a ray screen from the fort.

"They fight with a wild viciousness now. They won't let a ship get near them. They destroy everything on sight. They seem tremendously afraid of that apparatus of yours. Too bad we had no more."

"We will have — if you will let me get to work."

They went to the ship, and entered it. Arcot senior did not follow, but the others waited, while the ship left Earth once more, and floated in space. Immediately they went into the time-field.

They worked steadily, sleeping when necessary, and the giant strength of Torlos was frequently as great an asset as his indefatigable work. He was learning rapidly, and was able to do a great deal of the work without direction. He was not a scientist, and the thing was new to him, but his position as one of the best of the secret intelligence force of Nansal had proven his brains, and he did his share.

The others, scientists all, found the operations difficult, for work had been allotted to each according to his utmost capabilities.

It was still nearly a week of their time before the apparatus was completed to the extent possible, less than a minute of normal time passing.

Finally the unassembled, but completed apparatus, was carried to the laboratory of the cottage, and word was sent to all the men of Earth that Arcot was going to give a demonstration of the apparatus he hoped would save them. The scientists from all over Earth and Venus were interested, and those of Earth came, for there was no time for the men of Venus to arrive to inspect the results.

CHAPTER XVII

POWER OF MIND

It was night. The stars visible through the laboratory windows winked violently in the disturbed air of the Heaviside layer, for the molecular ray screen was still up.

The laboratory was dimly lighted now, all save the front of the room. There, a mass of compact boxes were piled one on another, and interconnected in various and indeterminate ways. And one table lay in a brilliant path of illumination. Behind it stood Arcot. He was talking to the dim white group of faces beyond the table, the scientists of Earth assembled.

"I have explained our power. It is the power of all the universe — Cosmic Power — which is necessarily vaster than all others combined.

"I cannot explain the control in the time I have at my disposal but the mathematics of it, worked out in two months of constant effort, you can follow from the printed work which will appear soon.

"The second thing, which some of you have seen before, has already been partly explained. It is, in brief, artificially created matter. The two important things to remember about it are that it *is*, that it *does exist*, and that it exists *only where it is determined to exist by the control there, and nowhere else.*

"These are all coordinated under the new mental relay control. Some of you will doubt this last, but think of it under this light. Will, thought, concentration — they are efforts, they require energy. Then they can exert energy! That is the key to the whole thing.

"But now for the demonstration."

Arcot looked toward Morey, who stood off to one side. There was a heavy thud as Morey pushed a small button. The relay had closed. Arcot's mind was now connected with the controls.

A globe of cloudiness appeared. It increased in density, and was a solid, opalescent sphere.

"There is a sphere, a foot in diameter, ten feet from me," droned Arcot. The sphere was there. "It is moving to the left." The sphere moved to the left at Arcot's thought. "It is rising." The sphere rose. "It is changing to a disc two feet across." The sphere seemed to flow, and was a disc two feet across as Arcot's toneless voice of concentration continued.

"It is changing into a hand, like a human hand." The disc changed into a human hand, the fingers slightly bent, the soft, white fingers of a woman with the pink of the flesh and the wrinkles at the knuckles visible. The wrist seemed to fade gradually into nothingness, the end of the hand was as indeterminate as are things in a dream, but the hand was definite.

"The hand is reaching for the bar of lux metal on the floor." The soft, little hand moved, and reached down and grasped the half ton bar of lux metal, wrapped dainty fingers about it and lifted it smoothly and effortlessly to the table, and laid it there.

A mistiness suddenly solidified to another hand. The second hand joined the first, and fell to work on the bar, and pulled. The bar stretched finally under an enormous load. One hand let go, and the thud of the highly elastic lux metal bar's return to its original shape echoed through the soundless room. These men of the twenty-second century knew what relux and lux metals were, and knew their enormous strength. Yet it was putty under these hands. The hands that looked like a woman's!

The bar was again placed on the table, and the hands disappeared. There was a thud, and the relay had opened.

"I can't demonstrate the power I have. It is impossible. The power is so enormous that nothing short of a sun could serve as a demonstration-hall. It is utterly beyond comprehension under any conditions. I have demonstrated artificial matter, and control by mental action.

"I'm now going to show you some other things we have learned. Remember, I can control perfectly the properties of artificial matter, by determining the structure it shall have.

"Watch."

Morey closed the relay. Arcot again set to work. A heavy ingot of iron was raised by a clamp that fastened itself upon it, coming from nowhere. The iron moved, and settled over the table. As it approached, a mistiness that formed became a crucible. The crucible showed the gray of pure iron, but it was artificial matter. The iron settled in the crucible, and a strange process of flowing began. The crucible became a ball, and colors flowed across its surface, till finally it was glowing richly silvery. The ball opened, and a great lump of silvery stuff was within it. It settled to the floor, and the ball disappeared, but the silvery metal did not.

"Platinum," said Morey softly. A gasp came from the audience. "Only platinum could exist there, and the matter had to rearrange itself as platinum." He could rearrange it in any form he chose, either absorbing or supplying energy of existence and energy of formation.

The mistiness again appeared in the air, and became a globe, a globe of brown. But it changed, and disappeared. Morey recognized the signal. "He will now make the artificial matter into all the elements, and many nonexistent elements, unstable, atomic figures." There followed a long series of changes.

The material shifted again, and again. Finally the last of the natural elements was left behind, all 104 elements known to man were shown, and many others.

"We will skip now. This is element of atomic weight 7000."

It was a lump of soft, oozy blackness. One could tell from the way that Arcot's mind handled it that it was soft. It seemed cold, terribly cold. Morey explained:

"It is very soft, for its atom is so large that it is soft in the molecular state. It is tremendously photoe-lectric, losing electrons very readily, and since its atom has so enormous a volume, its electrons are very far from the nucleus in the outer rings, and they absorb rays of very great length; even radio and some shorter audio waves seem to affect it. That accounts for its blackness, and the softness as Arcot has truly depicted it. Also, since it absorbs heat waves and changes them to electrical charges, it tends to become cold, as the frost Arcot has shown indicates. Remember, that that is infinitely hard as you see it, for it is artificial matter, but Arcot has seen natural matter forced into this exceedingly explosive atomic figuration.

"It is so heavily charged in the nucleus that its X-ray spectrum is well toward the gamma! The inner electrons can scarcely vibrate."

Again the substance changed — and was gone.

"Too far — atom of weight 20,000 becomes invisible and nonexistent as space closes in about it — perhaps the origin of our space. Atoms of this weight, if breaking up, would form two or more atoms that would exist in our space, then these would be unstable, and break down further into normal atoms. We don't know.

"And one more substance," continued Morey as he opened the relay once more. Arcot sat down and rested his head in his hands. He was not accustomed to this strain, and though his mind was one of the most powerful on Earth, it was very hard for him.

"We have a substance of commercial and practical use now. Cosmium. Arcot will show one method of making it."

Arcot resumed his work, seated now. A formation reached out, and grasped the lump of platinum still on the floor. Other bars of iron were brought over from the stack of material laid ready, and piled on a broad sheet that had formed in the air, tons of it, tens of tons. Finally he stopped. There was enough. The sheet wrapped itself into a sphere, and contracted, slowly, steadily. It was rampant with energy, energy flowed from it, and the air about was glowing with ionization. There was a feeling of awful power that seeped into the minds of the watchers, and held them spellbound before the glowing, opalescent sphere. The tons of matter were compressed now to a tiny ball! Suddenly the energy flared out violently, a terrific burst of energy, ionizing the air in the entire room, and shooting it with tiny, burning sparks. Then it was over. The ball split, and became two planes. Between them was a small ball of a glistening solid. The planes moved slowly together, and the ball flattened, and flowed. It was a sheet.

A clamp of artificial matter took it, and held the paper-thin sheet, many feet square, in the air. It seemed it must bend under its own enormous weight of tons, but thin as it was it did not.

"Cosmium," said Morey softly.

Arcot crumpled it, and pressed it once more between artificial matter tools. It was a plate, thick as heavy cardboard, and two feet on a side. He set it in a holder of artificial matter, a sort of frame, and caused the controls to lock.

Taking off the headpiece he had worn, he explained, "As Morey said, Cosmium. Briefly, density, 5007.89. Tensile strength, about two hundred thousand times that of good steel!" The audience gasped. That seems little to men who do not realize what it meant. An inch of this stuff would be harder to penetrate than three miles of steel!

"Our new ship," continued Arcot, "will carry six-inch armor. Six inches would be the equivalent of eighteen miles of solid steel, with the enormous improvement that it will be concentrated, and so will have far greater resistance than any amount of steel. Its tensile strength would be the equivalent of an eighteen-mile wall of steel.

"But its most important properties are that it reflects everything we know of. Cosmics, light, and even moleculars! It is made of cosmic ray photons, as lux is made of light photons, but the inexpressibly tighter bond makes the strength enormous. It cannot be handled by any means save by artificial matter tools.

"And now I am going to give a demonstration of the theatrical possibilities of this new agent. Hardly scientific — but amusing."

But it wasn't exactly amusing.

Arcot again donned the headpiece. "I think," he continued,

"that a manifestation of the super-natural will be most interesting. Remember that all you see is real, and all effects are produced by artificial matter generated by the cosmic energy, as I have explained, and are controlled by my mind."

Arcot had chosen to give this demonstration with definite reason. Apparently a bit of scientific playfulness, yet he knew that nothing is so impressive, nor so lastingly remembered as a theatrical demonstration of science. The greatest scientist likes to play with his science.

But Arcot's experiment now — it was on a level of its own!

From behind the table, apparently crawling up the leg came a thing! It was a hand. A horrible, disjointed hand. It was withered and incarmined with blood, for it was severed from its wrist, and as it hunched itself along, moving by a ghastly twitching of fingers and thumb, it left a trail of red behind it. The papers to be distributed rustled as it passed, scurrying suddenly across the table, down the leg, and racing toward the light switch! By some process of writhing jerks it reached it, and suddenly the room was plunged into half-light as the lights winked out. Light filtering over the transom of the door from the hall alone illuminated the hall, but the hand glowed! It glowed, and scurried away with an awful rustling, scuttling into some unseen hole in the wall. The quiet of the hall was the quiet of tenseness.

From the wall, coming through it, came a mistiness that solidified as it flowed across. It was far to the right, a bent stooped figure, a figure half glimpsed, but fully known, for it carried in its bony, glowing hand a great, nicked scythe. Its rattling tread echoed hollowly on the floor. Stooping walk, shuffling gait, the great metal scythe scraping on the floor, half seen as the gray, luminous cloak blew open in some unfelt breeze of its ephemeral world, revealing bone; dry, gray bone. Only the scythe seemed to know Life, and it was red with that Life. Slow running, sticky lifestuff.

Death paused, and raised his awful head. The hood fell back from the cavernous eyesockets, and they flamed with a greenish radiance that made every strained face in the room assume the same deathly pallor.

"The Scythe, the Scythe of Death," grated the rusty Voice. "The Scythe is slow, too slow. I bring new things," it cackled in its cracked voice, "new things of my tools. See!" The clutching bones dropped the rattling Scythe, and the handle broke as it fell, and rotted before their eyes. "Heh, heh," the Thing cackled as it watched. "Heh — what Death touches, rots as he leaves it." The grinning, blackened skull grinned wider, in an awful, leering cavity, rotting, twisted teeth showed. But from under his flapping robe, the skeletal hands drew something — ray pistols!

"These — these are swifter!" The Thing turned, and with a single leering glance behind, flowed once more through the wall.

A gasp, a stifled, groaning gasp ran through the hall, a half sob.

But far, far away they could hear something clanking, dragging its slow way along. Spellbound they turned to the farthest corner — and looked down the long, long road that twined off in distance. A lone, luminous figure plodded slowly along it, his half human shamble bringing him rapidly nearer.

Larger and larger he loomed, clearer and clearer became the figure, and his burden. Broken, twisted steel, or metal of some sort, twisted and blackened.

"It's over — it's over — and my toys are here. I win, I always win. For I am the spawn of Mars, of War, and of Hate, the sister of War, and my toys are the things they leave behind." It gesticulated, waving the twisted stuff and now through the haze, they could see them — buildings. The framework of buildings and twisted liners, broken weapons.

It loomed nearer, the cavernous, glowing eyes under low, shaggy brows, became clear, the awful brutal hate, the lust of Death, the rotting flesh of Disease — all seemed stamped on the Horror that approached.

"Ah!" It had seen them! "Ahh!" It dropped the buildings, the broken things, and shuffled into a run, toward them! Its face changed, the lips drew back from broken, stained teeth, the curling, cruel lips, and the rotting flesh of the face wrinkled into a grin of lust and hatred. The shaggy mop of its hair seemed to writhe and twist, the long, thin fingers grasped spasmodically as it neared. The torn, broken fingernails were visible — nearer — nearer — nearer —

"Oh, God — stop it!" A voice shrieked out of the dark as someone leaped suddenly to his feet.

Simultaneously with the cry the Thing puffed into nothingness of energy from which it had sprung, and a great ball of clear, white glowing light came into being in the center of the room, flooding it with a light that dazzled the eyes, but calmed broken nerves.

CHAPTER XVIII

EARTH'S DEFENSES

"I am sorry, Arcot. I did not know, for I see I might have helped, but to me, with my ideas of horror, it was as you said, amusement," said Torlos. They were sitting now in Arcot's study at the cottage; Arcot, his father, Morey, Wade, Torlos, the three Ortolians and the Talsonian.

"I know, Torlos. You see, where I made my mistake, as I have said, was in forgetting that in doing as I did, picturing horror, like a snowball rolling, it would grow greater. The idea of horror, started, my mind pictured one, and it inspired greater horror, which in turn reacted on my all too reactive apparatus. As you said, the things changed as you watched, molding themselves constantly as my mind changed them, under its own initiative and the concentrated thoughts of all those others. It was a very foolish thing to do, for that last Thing — well, remember it *was*, it existed, and the idea of hate and lust it portrayed was caused by my mind, but my mind could picture what it would do, if such were its emotions, and it would do them because my mind pictured them! And *nothing* could resist it!" Arcot's face was white once more as he thought of the danger he had run, of the terrible consequences possible of that 'amusement.'

"I think we had best start on the ship. I'll go get some sleep now, and then we can go."

Arcot led the way to the ship, while Torlos, Morey and Wade and Stel Felso Theu accompanied him. The Ortolians were to work on Earth, aiding in the detection of attacks by means of their mental investigation of the enemy.

"Well — good-bye, Dad. Don't know when I'll be back. Maybe twenty-five thousand years from now, or twenty-five thousand years ago. But we'll get back somehow. And we'll clean out the Thessians!"

He entered the ship, and rose into space.

"Where are you going, Arcot?" asked Morey.

"Eros," replied Arcot laconically.

"Not if my mind is working right," cried Wade suddenly. All the others were tense, listening for inaudible sounds.

"I quite agree," replied Arcot. The ship turned about, and dived toward New York, a hundred thousand miles behind now, at a speed many times that of light as Arcot snapped into time.

Across the void, Zezdon Fentes' call had come — New York was to be attacked by the Thessians, New York and Chicago next. New York because the orbits of their two forts were converging over that city in a few minutes!

They were in the atmosphere, screaming through it as their relux glowed instantaneously in the Heaviside layer, then was through before damage could be done. The screen was up.

Scarcely a minute after they passed, the entire heavens blazed into light, the roar of tremendous thunders crashing above them, great lightning bolts rent the upper air for miles as enormous energies clashed.

"Ah — they are sending everything they have against that screen, and it's hot. We have ten of our biggest tube stations working on it, and more coming in, to our total of thirty, but they have two forts, and Lord knows how many ships.

"I think me I'm going to cause them some worrying."

Arcot turned the ship, and drove up again, now at a speed very low to them but as they had the time-field up, very great. They passed the screen, and a tremendous bolt struck the ship. Everything in it was shielded, but the static was still great enough to cause them some trouble as the time-field and electric field fought. But the time-field, because of its very nature, could work faster, and they won through undamaged, though the enormous current seemed flowing for many minutes as they drifted slowly past it. Slowly — at fifty miles a second.

Out in space, free of the atmosphere, Arcot shot out to the point where the Thessians were congregating. The shining dots of their ships and the discs of the forts were visible from Earth save for the air's distortion.

They seemed a miniature Milky Way, their deadly beams concentrated on Earth.

Then the Thessians discovered that the terrestrial fleet was in action. A ship glowed with the ray, the opalescence of relux under moleculars visible on its walls. It simply searched for its opponent while its relux slowly yielded. It found it in time, and the terrestrial ship put up its screen.

The terrestrial fleet set to work, everything they had flying at the Thessian giants, but the Thessians had heavier ships, and heavier tubes. More power was winning for them. Inevitably, when the Sun's interference somewhat weakened the ray shield —

About that time Arcot arrived. The nearest fort dived toward the further with an acceleration that smashed it against no less than ten of its own ships before they could so much as move.

When the way was clear to the other fort — and that fort had moved, the berserk fort started off a new tack — and garnered six more wrecks on its side.

Then Thett's emissaries located Arcot. The screen was up, and the Negrian attractive ray apparatus which Arcot had used was working through it. The screen flashed here and there and collapsed under the full barrage of half the Thessian fleet, as Arcot had suspected it would. But the same force that made it collapse operated a relay that turned on the space control, and Thett's molecular ray energy steamed off to outer space.

"We worried them, then dug our hole and dragged it in after us, as usual, but damn it, we can't hurt them!" said Arcot disgustedly. "All we can do is tease them, then go hide where it's perfectly safe, in artificial —" Arcot stopped in amazement. The ship had been held under such space control that space was shut in about them, and they were motionless. The dials had reached a steady point, the current flow had become zero, and they hung there with only the very slow drain of the Sun's gravitational field and that of the planet's field pulling on the ship. Suddenly the current had leaped, and the dials giving the charge in the various coil banks had moved them down toward zero.

"Hey — they've got a wedge in here and are breaking out our hole. Turn on all the generators, Morey." Arcot was all action now. Somehow, inconceivable though it was, the Thessians had spotted them, and got some means of attacking them, despite their invulnerable position in another space!

The generators were on, pouring enormous power into the coils, and the dials surged, stopped, and climbed ever so slowly. They should have jumped back under that charge, ordinarily dangerously heavy. For perhaps thirty seconds they climbed, then they started down at full speed!

Arcot's hand darted to the time field, and switched it on full. The dial jerked, swung, then swung back, and started falling in unison with the dials, stopped, and climbed. All climbed swiftly, gaining ever more rapidly. With what seemed a jerk, the time dial flew over, and back, as Arcot opened the switch. They were free, and the dial on the space control coils was climbing normally now.

"By the Nine Planets, did they drink out our energy! The energy of six tons of lead just like that!"

"How'd they do it?" asked Wade.

Torlos kept silent, and helped Morey replace the coils of lead wire with others from stock.

"Same way we tickled them," replied Arcot, carefully studying the control instruments, "with the gravity ray! We knew all along that gravitational fields drank out the energy — they simply pulled it out faster than we could pump it in, and used four different rays on us doing it. Which speaks well for a little ship! But they burned off the relux on one room here, and it's a wreck. The molecs hit everything in it. Looks like something bad," called Arcot. The room was Morey's, but he'd find that out himself. "In the meantime, see if you can tell where we are. I got loose from their rays by going on both the high speed time-field and the space control at full, with all generators going full blast. Man, they had a stranglehold on us that time! But wait till we get that new ship turned out!"

With the telectroscope they could see what was happening. The terrific bombardment of rays was continuing, and the fleets were locked now in a struggle, the combined fleets of Earth and Venus and of Nansal, far across the void. Many of the terrestrian, or better, Solarian ships, were equipped with space distortion apparatus, now, and had some measure of safety in that the attractive rays of the Thessians could not be so concentrated on them. In numbers was safety; Arcot had been endangered because he was practically alone at the time they attacked.

But it was obvious that the Solarian fleet was losing. They could not compete with the heavier ships, and now the frequent flaming bursts of light that told of a ship caught in the new deadly ray showed another danger.

"I think Earth is lost if you cannot aid it soon, Arcot, for other Thessian ships are coming," said Stel Felso Theu softly.

From out of the plane of the planetary orbits they were coming, across space from some other world, a fleet of dozens of them. They were visible as one after another leapt into normal time-rates.

"Why don't they fight in advanced time?" asked Morey, half aloud.

"Because the genius that designed that apparatus didn't think of it. Remember, Morey, those ships have their time apparatus connected with their power apparatus so that the power has to feed the time continuously. They have no coils like ours. When they advance their time, they're weakened every other way."

"We need that new ship. Are we going to make it?" demanded Arcot.

"Take weeks at best. What chance?" asked Morey.

"Plenty; watch." As he spoke, Arcot pulled open the time controls, and spun the ship about. They headed off toward a tiny point of light far beyond. It rushed toward them, grew with the swiftness of an exploding bomb, and was suddenly a great, rough fragment of a planet hanging before them, miles in extent.

"Eros," explained Wade laconically to Torlos. "Part of an ancient planet that was destroyed before the time of man, or life on Earth. The planet got too near the sun when its orbit was irregular, and old Sol pulled it to pieces. This is one of the pieces. The other asteroids are the rest. All planetary surfaces are made up of great blocks; they aren't continuous, you know. Like blocks of concrete in a building, they can slide a bit on each other, but friction holds them till they slip with a jar and we have earthquakes. This is one of the planetary blocks. We see Eros from Earth intermittently, for when this thing turns broadside it reflects a lot of light; edge on it does not reflect so much."

It was a desolate bit of rock. Bare, airless, waterless rock, of enormous extent. It was contorted and twisted, but there were no great cracks in it for it was a single planetary block.

Arcot dropped the ship to the barren surface, and anchored it with an attractive ray at low concentration. There was no gravity of consequence on this bit of rock.

"Come on, get to work. Space suits, and rush all the apparatus out," snapped Arcot. He was on his feet, the power of the ship in neutral now. Only the attractor was on. In the shortest possible time they got into their suits, and under Arcot's direction set up the apparatus on the rocky soil as fast as it was brought out. In all, less than fifteen minutes were needed, yet Arcot was hurrying them more and more. Torlos' tremendous strength helped, even on this gravitationless world, for he could accelerate more quickly with his burdens.

At last it was up for operation. The artificial matter apparatus was operated by cosmic power, and controlled by mental operation, or by mathematical formula as they pleased. Immediately Arcot set to work. A giant hollow cylinder drilled a great hole completely through the thin, curved surface of the ancient planetary block, through twelve miles of solid rock — a cylinder of artificial matter created on a scale possible only to cosmic power. The cylinder, half a mile across, contained a huge plug of matter. Then the artificial matter contracted swiftly, compressing the matter, and simultaneously treating it with the tremendous fields that changed its energy form. In seconds it was a tremendous mass of cosmium.

A second smaller cylinder bored a plug from the rock, and worked on it. A huge mass of relux resulted. Now other artificial matter tools set to work at Arcot's bidding, and cut pieces from his huge masses of raw materials, and literally, quick as thought, built a great framework of them, anchored in the solid rock of the planetoid.

Then a tremendous plane of matter formed, and neatly bisected the planetoid, two great flat pieces of rock were left where one had been — miles across, miles thick — planetary chips.

On the great framework that had been constructed, four tall shafts of cosmium appeared, and each was a hollow tube, up the center of which ran a huge cable of relux. At the peak of each mile-high shaft was a great globe. Now in the framework below things were materializing as Arcot's flying thoughts arranged them — great tubes of cosmium with relux element — huge coils of relux conductors, insulated with microscopic but impenetrable layers of cosmium.

Still, for all his swiftness of mind and accuracy of thought, he had to correct two mistakes in all his work. It was nearly an hour before the thing was finished. Then, two hundred feet long, a hundred wide, and fifty in height, the great mechanism was completed, the tall columns rising from four corners of the greater framework that supported it.

Then, into it, Arcot turned the powers of the cosmos. The stars in the airless space wavered and danced as though seen through a thick atmosphere. Tingling power ran through them as it flowed into the tremendous coils. For thirty seconds — then the heavens were as before.

At last Arcot spoke. Through the radio communicators, and through the thought-channels, his ideas came as he took off the headpiece. "It's done now, and we can rest." There was a tremendous crash from within the apparatus. The heavens reeled before them, and shifted, then were still, but the stars were changed. The sun shone weirdly, and the stars were altered.

"That is a time shifting apparatus on a slightly larger scale," replied Arcot to Torlos' question, "and is designed to give us a chance to work. Come on, let's sleep. A week here should be a few minutes of Earthtime."

"You sleep, Arcot. I'll prepare the materials for you," suggested Morey. So Arcot and Wade went to sleep, while Morey and the Talsonian and Torlos worked. First Morey bound the *Ancient Mariner* to the frame of the time apparatus, safely away from the four luminous balls, broadcasters of the time field. Then he shut off the attractive ray, and bound himself in the operator's seat of the apparatus of the artificial matter machine.

A plane of artificial matter formed, and a stretch of rock rose under its lift as it cleft the rock apart. A great cleared, level space resulted. Other artificial matter enclosed the rock, and the fragments cut free were treated under tremendous pressure. In a few moments a second enormous mass of cosmium was formed.

For three hours Morey worked steadily, building a tremendous reserve of materials. Lux metal he did not make, but relux, the infusible, perfect conductor, and cosmium in tremendous masses, he did make. And he made some great blocks of oxygen from the rock, transmuting the atoms, and stored it frozen on the plane, with liquid hydrogen in huge tanks, and some metals that would be needed. Then he slept while they waited for Arcot.

Eight hours after he had lain down, Arcot was up, and ate his breakfast. He set to work at once with the machine. It didn't suit him, it seemed, and first he made a new tool, a small ship that could move about, propelled by a piece of artificial matter, and the entire ship was a tremendously greater artificial matter machine, with a greater power than before!

His thoughts, far faster than hands could move, built up the gigantic hull of the new ship, and put in the rooms, and the brace members in less than twelve hours. A titanic shell of eight-inch cosmium, a space, with braces of the same nonconductor of heat, cosmium, and a two inch inner hull. A tiny space in the gigantic hull, a space less than one thousand cubic feet in dimension was the control and living quarters.

It was held now on great cosmium springs, but Arcot was not by any means through. One man must do all the work, for one brain must design it, and though he received the constant advice and help of Morey and the others, it was his brain that pictured the thing that was built.

At last the hull was completed. A single, glistening tube, of enormous bulk, a mile in length, a thousand feet in diameter. Yet nearly all of that great bulk would be used immediately. Some room would be left for additional apparatus they might care to install. Spare parts they did not have to carry — they could make their own from the energy abounding in space.

The enormous, shining hull was a thing of beauty through stark grandeur now, but obviously incomplete. The ray projectors were not mounted, but they were to be ray projectors of a type never before possible. Space is the transmitter of all rays, and it is in space that those energy forms exist. Arcot had merely to transfer the enormously high energy level of the space-curvature to any form of energy he wanted, and now, with the complete statistics on it, he was able to do that directly. No tubes, no genera-tors, only fields that changed the energy already there — the immeasurable energy available!

The next period of work he started the space distortion appa-ratus. That must go at the exact center of the ship. One tremen-dous coil, big enough for the *Ancient Mariner* to lie in easily! Minutes, and flying thoughts had made it — then came thousands of the individual coils, by thinking of one, and picturing it many times! In ranks, rows, and columns they were piled into a great block, for power must be stored for use of this tremendous machine, while in the artificial space when its normal power was not available, and that power source must be tremendous.

Then the time apparatus, and after that the driving apparatus. Not the molecular drive now, but an attraction ray focused on their own ship, with projectors scattered about the ship that it might move effortlessly in every direction. And provision was made for a force-drive by means of artificial matter, planes of it pushing the ship where it was wanted. But with the attraction-drive they would be able to land safely, without fear of being crushed by their own weight on Thett, for all its enormous gravity.

The control was now suspended finally, with a series of attrac-tion drives about it, locking it immovably in place, while smaller attraction devices stimulated gravity for the occupants.

Then finally the main apparatus — the power plant — was installed. The enormous coils which handled, or better, caused space to handle as they directed, powers so great that whole suns could be blasted instantaneously, were put in place, and the field generators that would make and direct their rays, their ray screen if need be, and handle their artificial matter. Everything was installed, and all but a rather small space was occupied.

It had been six weeks of continuous work for them, for the mind of each was aiding in this work, indirectly or directly, and it neared completion now.

"But, we need one more thing, Arcot. That could never land on any planet smaller than Jupiter. What is its mass?" suggested Morey.

"Don't know, I'm sure, but it is of the order of a billion tons. I know you are right. What are we going to do?"

"Put on a tender."

"Why not the *Ancient Mariner*?" asked Wade.

"It isn't fitting. It was designed for individual use anyway," replied Morey. "I suggest something more like this on a small scale. We won't have much work on that, merely think of every detail of the big ship on a small scale, with the exception of the control cube furnishings. Instead of the numerous decks, swimming pool and so forth, have a large, single room."

"Good enough," replied Arcot.

As if by magic, a machine appeared, a "small" machine of two-hundred-foot length, modified slightly in some parts, its bottom flattened, and equipped with an attractor anchor. Then they were ready.

"We will leave the *Mariner* here, and get it later. This apparatus won't be needed any longer, and we don't want the enemy to get it. Our trial trip will be a fight!" called Arcot as he leaped from his seat. The mass of the giant ship pulled him, and he fell slowly toward it.

Into its open port he flew, the others behind him, their suits still on. The door shut behind them as Arcot, at the controls, closed it. As yet they had not released the air supplies. It was airless.

Now the hiss of air, and the quickening of heat crept through it. The water in the tanks thawed as the heat came, soaking through from the great heaters. In minutes the air and heat were normal throughout the great bulk. There was air in power compartments, though no one was expected to go there, for the control room alone need be occupied; vision-screens here viewed every part of the ship, and all about it.

The eyes of the new ship were set in recesses of the tremendously strong cosmium wall, and over them, protecting them, was an infinitely thin, but infinitely strong wall of artificial matter, permanently maintained. It was opaque to all forms of radiation known from the longest Hertzian to the shortest cosmics, save for the very narrow band of visible light. Whether this protection would stop the Thessian beam that was so deadly to lux and relux was not, of course, known. But Arcot hoped it would, and, if that beam was radiant energy, or material particles, it would.

"We'll destroy our station here now, and leave the *Ancient Mariner* where it is. Of course we are a long way out of the orbit this planetoid followed, due to the effect of the time apparatus, but we can note where it is, and we'll be able to find it when we want it," said Arcot, seated at the great control board now. There were no buttons now, or visible controls; all was mental.

A tiny sphere of artificial matter formed, and shot toward the control board of the time machine outside. It depressed the main switch, and space about them shifted, twisted, and returned to normal. The time apparatus was off for the first time in six weeks.

"Can't fuse that, and we can't crush it. It's made of cosmium, and trying to crush it against the rock would just drive it into it. We'll see what we can do though," muttered Arcot. A plane of artificial matter formed just beneath it, and sheared it from its bed on the planetoid, cutting through the heavy cosmium anchors. The framework lifted, and the apparatus with it. A series of planes, a gigantic honeycomb formed, and the apparatus was cut across again and again, till only small fragments were left of it. Then these were rolled into a ball, and crushed by a sphere of artificial matter beyond all repair. The enemy would never learn their secret.

A huge cylinder of artificial matter cut a great gouge from the plane that was left where the apparatus had been, and a clamp of the same material picked up the *Ancient Mariner*, deposited it there, then covered it with rubble and broken rock. A cosmic flashed on the rock for an instant, and it was glowing, incandescent lava. The *Ancient Mariner* was buried under a hundred feet of rapidly solidifying rock, but rock which could be fused away from its infusible walls when the time came.

"We're ready to go now — get to work with the radio, Morey, when we get to Earth."

The gravity seemed normal here as they walked about, no accelerations affected them as the ship darted forward, for all its inconceivably great mass, like an arrow, then flashed forward under time control. The sun was far distant now, for six weeks they had been traveling with the section of Eros under time control. But with their tremendous time control plant, and the space control, they reached the solar system in very little time.

It seemed impossible to them that that battle could still be waging, but it was. The ships of Earth and Venus, battling now as a last, hopeless stand, over Chicago, were attempting to stop the press of a great Thessian fleet. Thin, long Negrian, or Sirian ships had joined them in the hour of Earth time that the men had been working. Still, despite the reinforcements, they were falling back.

CHAPTER XIX

THE BATTLE OF EARTH

It had been an anxious hour for the forces of the Solar System.

They were in the last fine stages of Earth's defense when the general staff received notice that a radio message of tremendous power had penetrated the ray screen, with advice for them. It was signed "Arcot."

"Bringing new weapon. Draw all ships within the atmosphere when I start action, and drive Thessians back into space. Retire as soon as a distance of ten thousand miles is reached. I will then handle the fleet," was the message.

"Gentlemen: We are losing. The move suggested would be eminently poor tactics unless we are sure of being able to drive them. If we don't, we are lost in any event. I trust Arcot. How vote you?" asked General Hetsar Sthel.

The message was relayed to the ships. Scarcely a moment after the message had been relayed, a tremendous battleship appeared in space, just beyond the battle. It shot forward, and planted itself directly in the midst of the battle, brushing aside two huge Thessians in its progress. The Thessian ships bounced off its sides, and reeled away. It lay waiting, making no move. All the Thessian ships above poured the full concentration of their moleculars into its tremendous bulk. A diffused glow of opalescence ran over every ship — save the giant. The moleculars were being reflected from its sides, and their diffused energy attacked the very ships that were sending them!

A fort moved up, and the deadly beam of destruction reached out, luminous even in space.

"Now," muttered Morey, "we shall see what cosmium will stand."

A huge spot on the side of the ship had become incandescent. A vapor, a strange puff of smokiness exploded from it, and disappeared instantly. Another came and faster and faster they followed each other. The cosmium was disintegrating under the ray, but very slowly, breaking first into gaseous cosmic rays, then free, and spreading.

"We will not fight," muttered Morey happily as he saw Arcot shift in his seat.

Arcot picked the moleculars. They reached out, touched the heavy relux of the fort, and it exploded into opalescence that was hazily white, the colors shifted so quickly. A screen sprang into being, and the ray was chopped off. The screen was a mass of darting flames as energies of stupendous magnitude clashed.

Arcot used a bit more of his inconceivable power. The ray struck the screen, and it flashed once — then died into blackness. The fort suddenly crumpled in like a dented can, and rolled clumsily away. The other fort was near now, and started an attack of its own. Arcot chose the artificial matter this time. He was not watching the many attacking ships.

The great ship careened suddenly, fell over heavily to one side. "Foolish of me," said Arcot. "They tried crashing us."

A mass of crumpled, broken relux and lux surrounded by a haze of gas lying against a slight scratch on the great sides, told the story. Eight inches of cosmium does not give way.

Yet another ship tried it. But it stopped several feet away from the real wall of the ship. It struck a wall even more unyielding — artificial matter.

But now Arcot was using this major weapon — artificial matter. Ship after ship, whether fleeing or attacking, was surrounded suddenly by a great sphere of it, a sudden terrific blaze of energy as the sphere struck the ray shield, the control forces now backed by the energy of all the millions of stars of space shattered it in an instant. Then came the inexorable crush of the artificial matter, and a ball of matter alone remained.

But the pressing disc of the battle-front which had been lowering on Chicago, greatest of Earth's metropolises, was lifted. This disc-front was staggering back now as Arcot's mighty ship weakened its strength, and destroyed its morale, under the steady drive of the now hopeful Solarians.

The other gigantic fort moved up now, with twenty of the largest battleships. The fort turned loose its destructive ray — and Arcot tried his new "magnet." It was not a true magnet, but a transformed space field, a field created by the energy of all the universe.

The fort was gigantic. Even Arcot's mighty ship was a small thing beside it, but suddenly it seemed warped and twisted as space curved visibly in a magnetic field of such terrific intensity as to be immeasurable.

Arcot's armory was tested and found not wanting.

Suddenly every Thessian ship in sight ceased to exist. They disappeared. Instantly Arcot threw on all time power, and darted toward Venus. The Thessians were already nearing the planet, and no possible rays could overtake them. An instantaneous touch of the space control, and the mighty ship was within hundreds of miles of the atmosphere.

Space twisted about them, reeled, and was firm. The Thessian fleet was before them in a moment, visible now as they slowed to normal speed. Startled, no doubt, to find before them the ship they had fled, they charged on for a space. Then, as though by some magic, they stopped and exploded in gouts of light.

When space had twisted, seconds before, it was because Arcot had drawn on the enormous power of space to an extent that had been appreciable even to it — ten sols. That was forty million tons of matter a second, and for a hundredth part of a second it had flowed. Before them, in a vast plane, had been created an infinitesimally thin film of artificial matter, four hundred thousand tons of it, and into this invisible, infinitely hard barrier, the Thessian fleet had rammed. And it was gone.

"I think," said Arcot softly, as he took off his headpiece, "that the beginning of the end is in sight."

"And I," said Morey, "think it is now out of sight. Half a dozen ships stopped. And they are gone now, to warn the others."

"What warning? What can they tell? Only that their ships were destroyed by something they couldn't see." Arcot smiled. "I'm going home."

CHAPTER XX

DESTRUCTION

Some time later, Arcot spoke. "I have just received a message from Zezdon Fentes that he has an important communication to make, so I will go down to New York instead of to Chicago, if you gentlemen do not mind. Morey will take you to Chicago in the tender, and I can find Zezdon Fentes."

Zezdon Fentes' message was brief. He had discovered from the minds of several who had been killed by the magnetic field Arcot had used, and not destroyed, that they had a base in this universe. Thett's base was somewhere near the center of the galaxy, on a system of unusually large planets, circling a rather small star. But what star their minds had not revealed.

"It's up to us then to locate said star," said Arcot, after listening to Zezdon Fentes' account: "I think the easiest way will be to follow them home. We can go to your world, Zezdon Fentes, and see what they are doing there, and drive them off. Then to yours, Stel Felso. I place your world second as it is far better able to defend itself than is Ortol. It is agreeable?"

It was, and the ship which had been hanging in the atmosphere over New York, where Zezdon Afthen, Fentes and Inthel had come to it in a taxi-ship, signaled for the crowd to clear away above. The enormous bulk of the shining machine, the savior of Earth, had attracted a very great amount of attention, naturally, and thousands on thousands of hardy souls had braved the cold of the fifteen mile height with altitude suits or in small ships. Now they cleared away, and as the ship slowly rose, the tremendous concentrated mental well-wishing of the thousands reached the men within the ship. "That," observed Morley, "is one thing cosmium won't stop. In some ways I wish it would — because the mental power that could be wielded by any great number of those highly advanced Thessians, if they know its possibilities, is not a thing to neglect."

"I can answer that, terrestrian," thought Zezdon Afthen. "Our instruments show great mental powers, and great ability to concentrate the will in mental processes, but they indicate a very slight development of these abilities. Our race, despite the fact that our mental powers are much less than those of such men as Arcot and yourself, have done, and can do many things your greater minds cannot, for we have learned the direction of the will. We need not fear the will of the Thessians. I feel confident of that!"

The ship was in space now, and as Arcot directed it toward Ortol, far far across the Island, he threw on, for the moment, the combined power of space distortion and time fields. Instantly the sun vanished, and when, less than a second later, he cut off the space field, and left only the time, the constellations were instantly recognizable. They were within a dozen light years of Ortol.

"Morey, may I ask what you call this machine?" asked Torlos.

"You may, but I can't answer," laughed Morey. "We were so anxious to get it going that we didn't name it. Any suggestions?"

For a moment none of them made any suggestions, then slowly came Arcot's thoughts, clear and sharp, the thoughts of carefully weighed decision.

"The swiftest thing that ever was *thought*! The most irresistible thing, *thought*, for nothing can stop its progress. The most destructive thing, *thought*. Thought, the greatest constructor, the greatest destroyer, the product of mind, and producer of powers, the greatest of powers. Thought is controlled by the mind. Let us call it *Thought*!"

"Excellent, Arcot, excellent. The *Thought*, the controller of the powers of the cosmos!" cried Morey.

"But the *Thought* has not been christened, save in battle, and then it had no name. Let us emblazen its name on it now," suggested Wade.

Stopping their motion through space, but maintaining a time field that permitted them to work without consuming precious time, Arcot formed some more cosmium, but now he subjected it to a special type of converted field, and into the cosmium, he forced some light photons, half bound, half free. The fixture he formed into the letters, and welded forever on the gigantic prow of the ship, and on its huge sides. *Thought*, it stood in letters ten feet high, made of clear transparent cosmium, and the golden light photons, imprisoned in it, the slowly disintegrating lux metal, would cause those letters to shine for countless aeons with the steady golden light they now had.

The *Thought* continued on now, and as they slowed their progress for Ortol, they saw that messengers of Thett had barely arrived. The fort here too had been razed to the ground, and now they were concentrating over the largest city of Ortol. Their rays were beating down on the great ray screen that terrestrial engineers had set up, protecting the city, as Earth had been protected. But the fleet that stood guard was small, and was rapidly being destroyed. A fort broke free, and plunged at last for the ray screen.

Its relux walls glowed a thousand colors as the tremendous energy of the ray-screen struck them — but it was through!

A molecular ray reached down for the city — and stopped halfway in a tremendous coruscating burst of light and energy. Yet there was none of the sheen of the ray screen. Merely light.

The fort was still driving downward. Then suddenly it stopped, and the side dented in like the side of a can some one has stepped on, and it came to sudden rest against an invisible, impenetrable barrier. A molecular reached down from somewhere in space, hit the ray screen of Ortol, which the Thessians had attacked for hours, and the screen flashed into sudden brilliance, and disappeared. The ray struck the Thessian fort, and the fort burst into tremendous opalescence, while the invisible barrier the ray had struck was suddenly a great sheet of flaming light. In less than half a second the opalescence was gone, the fort shuddered, and shrieked out of the planet's atmosphere, a mass of lux now, and susceptible to the moleculars. And everything that lived within that fort had died instantly and painlessly.

The fleet which had been preparing to follow the leading fort was suddenly stopped; it halted indecisively.

Then the *Thought* became visible as its great golden letters showed suddenly, streaking up from distant space. Every ship turned cosmic and moleculars on it. The cosmic rebounded from the cosmium walls, and from the artificial matter that protected the eyes. The moleculars did not affect either, but the invisible protective sheet that the *Thought* was maintaining in the Ortolian atmosphere became misty as it fought the slight molecular rebounds.

The *Thought* went into action. The fort which remained was the point of attack. The fort had turned its destructive ray on the cosmium ship with the result that, as before, the cosmium slowly disintegrated into puffs of cosmic rays. The vapor seemed to boil out, puff suddenly, then was gone. Arcot put up a wall of artificial matter to test the effect. The ray went right through the matter, without so much as affecting it. He tried a sheet of pure energy, an electro-magnetic energy stream of tremendous power. The ray bent sharply to one side. But in a moment the Thessians had realigned it.

"It's a photonic stream, but of some type that doesn't affect ordinary matter, but only artificial matter such as lux, relux, or cosmium. If the artificial matter would only fight it, I'd be all right." The thought running through Arcot's mind reached the others.

A tremendous burst of light energy to the rear announced the fact that a Thessian had crashed against the artificial matter wall that surrounded the ship. Arcot was throwing the Thessian destructive beam from side to side now, and twice succeeded in misdirecting it so that it hit the enemy machines.

The *Thought* sent out its terrific beam of magnetic energy. The ray was suddenly killed, and the fort cruised helplessly on. Its driving apparatus was dead. The diffused cosmic reached out, and as the magnetic field, the relux and the cosmics interacted, the great fort was suddenly blue-white — then instantly a dust that scattered before an enormous blast of air.

From the *Thought* a great shell of artificial matter went, a visible, misty wall, that curled forward, and wrapped itself around the Thessian ships with a motion of tremendous speed, yet deceptive, for it seemed to billow and flow.

A Thessian warship decided to brush it away — and plowed into inconceivable strength. The ship crumpled to a mass of broken relux.

The greater part of the Thessian fleet had already fled, but there remained half a hundred great battleships. And now, within half a million miles of the planet, there began a battle so weird that astronomers who watched could not believe it.

From behind the *Thought*, where it hung motionless beyond the misty wall, a Thing came.

The Thessian ships had realized now that the misty sphere that walled them in was impenetrable, and their rays were off, for none they now had would penetrate it. The forts were gone.

But the Thing that came behind the *Thought* was a ship, a little ship of the same misty white, and it flowed into, and through the wall, and was within their prison. The Thessian ships turned their rays toward it, and waited. What was this thing?

The ovaloid ship which drifted so slowly toward them suddenly seemed to jerk, and from it reached pseudopods! An amoeba on a titanic scale! It writhed its way purposefully toward the nearest ship, and while that ship waited, a pseudopod reached out, and suddenly drove through the four foot relux armor! A second pseudopod followed with lightning rapidity, and in an instant the ship had been split from end to end!

Now a hundred rays were leaping toward the thing, and the rays burst into fire and gouts of light, blackened, burned pseudopods seemed to fall from the thing and hastily it retreated from the enclosure, flowing once more through the wall that stopped their rays.

But another Thing came. It was enormous, a mile long, a great, shining scaly thing, a dragon, and on its mighty neck was mounted an enormous, distorted head, with great flat nose and huge flapping nostrils. It was a Thessian head! The mouth, fifty feet across, wrinkled into an horrific grin, and broken, stained teeth of iron showed in the mouth. Great talons upraised, it rent the misty wall that bound them, and writhed its awful length in. The swish of its scales seemed to come to the watchers, as it chased after a great battleship whose pilot fled in terror. Faster than the mighty spaceship the awful Thing caught it in mighty talons that ripped through solid relux. Scratching, fluttering enormous, blood-red wings, the silvery claws tore away great masses of relux, sending them flying into space.

Again rays struck at it. Cosmic and moleculars with blinding pencils of light. For now in the close space of the Wall was an atmosphere, the air of two great warships, and though the space was great, the air in the ships was dense.

The rays struck its awful face. The face burst into light, and black, greasy smoke steamed up, as the thing writhed and twisted horribly, awful screams ringing out. Then it was free, and half the face was burned away, and a grinning, bleeding, half-cooked face writhed and screamed in anger at them. It darted at the nearest ship, and ripped out that ray that burned it — and quivered into death. It quivered, then quickly faded into mist, a haze, and was gone!

A last awful thing — a thing they had not noticed as all eyes watched that Thing — was standing by the rent in the Sphere now, the gigantic Thessian, with leering, bestial jaws, enormous, squat limbs, the webbed fingers and toes, and the heavy torso of his race, grinning at them. In one hand was a thing — and his jaws munched. Thett's men stared in horror as they recognized that thing in his hand — a Thessian body! He grinned happily and reached for a battleship — a ray burned him. He howled, and leaped into their midst.

Then the Thessians went mad. All fought, and they fought each other, rays of all sorts, their moleculars and their cosmics, while in their midst the Giant howled his glee, and laughed and laughed —

Eventually it was over, and the last limping Thessian ship drove itself crazily against the wreck of its last enemy. And only wreckage was left.

"Lord, Arcot! Why in the Universe did you do that — and how did you conceive those horrors?" asked Morey, more than a little amazed at the tactics Arcot had displayed.

Arcot shook himself, and disconnected his controls. "Why — why I don't know. I don't know what made me do that, I'm sure. I never imagined anything like that dragon thing — how did —"

His keen eyes fixed themselves suddenly on Zezdon Fentes, and their tremendous hypnotic power beat down the resistance of the Ortolian's trained mind. Arcot's mind opened for the others the thoughts of Zezdon Fentes.

He had acted as a medium between the minds of the Thessians, and Arcot. Taking the horror-ideas of the Thessians, he had imprinted them on Arcot's mind while Arcot was at work with the controls. In Arcot's mind, they had acted exactly as had the ideas that night on Earth, only here the demonstration had been carried to the limit, and the horror ideas were compounded to the utmost. The Thessians, highly developed minds though they were, were not resistant and they had broken. The Allies, with their different horror-ideas, had been but slightly affected.

"We will leave you on Ortol, Zezdon Fentes. We know you have done much, and perhaps your own mind has given a bit. We hope you recover. I think you agree with me, Zezdon Afthen and Inthel?" thought Arcot.

"We do, heartily, and are heartily sorry that one of our race has acted in this way. Let us proceed to Talso, as soon as possible. You might send Fentes down in a shell of artificial matter," suggested Zezdon Afthen.

"Which," said Arcot, after this had been done, and they were on their way to Talso, "shows the danger of a mad *Thought!*"

CHAPTER XXI

THE POWER OF "*THE THOUGHT*"

But it seemed, or must have seemed to any infinite being capable of watching it as it moved now, that the *Thought* was a mad thought. With the time control opened to the limit, and a touch of the space control, it fled across the Universe at a velocity such as no other thing was capable of.

One star — it flashed to a disc, loomed enormous — overpowering — then suddenly they were flashing *through* it! The enormous coils fed their current into the space-coils and the time field, and the ship seemed to twist and writhe in distorted space as the gravitational field of a giant star, and a giant ship's space field fought for a fraction of time so short as to be utterly below measurement. Then the ship was gone — and behind it a star, the center of which had suddenly been hurled into another space forever, as the counteracting, gravitational field of the outer layers was removed for a moment, and only its own enormous density affected space, writhed and collapsed upon itself, to explode into a mighty sea of flames. Planets it formed, we know, by a process such as can happen when only this man-made accident happens.

But the ship fled on, its great coils partly discharged, but still far more charged than need be.

It was minutes to Talso where it had been hours with the *Ancient Mariner*, but now they traveled with the speed of *Thought*!

Talso too was the scene of a battle, and more of a battle than Ortol had been, for here where more powerful defensive forces had been active, the Thessians had been more vengeful. All their remaining ships seemed concentrated here. And the great molecular screen that terrestrian engineers had flung up here had already fallen. Great holes had opened in it, as two great forts, and a thousand ships, some mighty battleships of the intergalactic spaces, some little scout cruisers, had turned their rays on the struggling defensive machines. It had held for hours, thanks to the tremendous tubes that Talso had in their power-distribution stations, but in the end had fallen, but not before many of their largest cities had been similarly defended, and the people of the others had scattered broadcast.

True, wherever they might be, a diffused molecular would find them and destroy all life save under the few screens, but if the Thessians once diffused their rays, without entering the atmosphere, the broken screen would once more be able to hold.

No fleet had kept the Thessian forces out of this atmosphere, but dozens of more adequately powered artificial matter bomb stations had taught Thett respect for Talso. But Talso's own ray screen had stopped their bombs. They could only send their bombs as high as the screen. They did not have Arcot's tremendous control power to maintain the matter without difficulty even beyond a screen.

At last the screen had fallen, and the Thessian ships, a hole once made, were able to move, and kept that hole always under them, though if it once were closed, they would again have the struggle to open it.

Exploding matter bombs had twice caused such spatial strains and ionized conditions as to come near closing it, but finally the Thessian fleet had arranged a ring of ships about the hole, and opened a cylinder of rays that reached down to the planet.

Like some gigantic plow the rays tore up mountains, oceans, glaciers and land. Tremendous chasms opened in straight lines as it plowed along. Unprotected cities flashed into fountains of rock and soil and steel that leaped upwards as the rays touched, and were gone. Protected cities, their screens blazing briefly under the enormous ray concentrations as the ships moved on, unheeding, stood safe on islands of safety amidst the destruction. Here in the lower air, where ions would be so plentiful, Thett did not try to break down the screens, for the air would aid the defenders.

Finally, as Thett's forces had planned, they came to one of the ionized layer ray-screen stations that was still projecting its cone of protective screening to the layer above. Every available ray was turned on that station, and, designed as it was for protecting part of a world, the station was itself protected, but slowly, slowly as its already heated tubes weakened their electronic emission, the disc of ions retreated more and more toward the station, as, like some splashing stream, the Thessian rays played upon it forcing it back. A rapidly accelerating retreat, faster and faster, as the disc changed from the dull red of normal defense to the higher and bluer quanta of failing, less complete defense, the disc of interference retreated.

Then, with a flash of light, and a roar as the soil below spouted up, the station was gone. It had failed.

Instantly the ring of ships expanded as the great screen was weakened by the withdrawal of this support. Wider was the path of destruction now as the forces moved on.

But high, high in the sky, far out of sight of the naked eye, was a tiny spot that was in reality a giant ship. It was flashing forward, and in moments it was visible. Then, as another deserted city vanished, it was above the Thessian fleet.

Their rays were directed downward through a hole that was even larger. A second station had gone with that city. But, as by magic, the hole closed up, and chopped their rays off with a decisiveness that startled them. The interference was so sharp now that not even the dullest of reds showed where their beams touched. The close interference was giving off only radio! In amazement they looked for this new station of such enormous power that their combined rays did not noticeably affect it. A world had been fighting their rays unsuccessfully. What single station could do this, if the many stations of the world could not? There was but one they knew of, and they turned now to search for the ship they knew must be there.

"No horrors this time; just clean, burning energy," muttered Arcot.

It was clean, and it was burning. In an instant one of the forts was a mass of opalescence that shifted so swiftly it was purest white, then rocketed away, lifeless, and no longer relux.

The other fort had its screen up, though its power, designed to withstand the attack of a fleet of enormous intergalactic, matter-driven, fighting ships lasted but an instant under the driving power of half a million million suns, concentrated in one enormous ray of energy. The sheer energy of the ray itself, molecular ray though it was, heated the material it struck to blinding incandescence even as it hurled it at a velocity close to that of light into outer space. With little sparkling flashes battleships of the void after giant cruisers flashed into lux, and vanished under the ray.

A tremendous combined ray of magnetism and cosmic ray energy replaced the molecular, and the ships exploded into a dust as fine as the primeval gas from which came all matter.

Sweeping energy, so enormous that the defenses of the ships did not even operate against it, shattered ship after ship, till the few that remained turned, and, faster than the pursuing energies could race through space, faster than light, headed for their base.

"That was fair fight; energy against energy," said Arcot delightedly, for his new toy, which made playthings of suns and fed on the cosmic energy of a universe, was behaving nicely, "and as I said, Stel Felso Theu, at the beginning of this war, the greater Power wins, always. And in our island here, I have five hundred thousand million separate power plants, each generating at the rate of decillions of ergs a second, backing this ship.

"Your world will be safe now, and we will head for our last

embattled ally, Sirius." The titanic ship turned, and disappeared from the view of the madly rejoicing billions of Talso below, as it sped, far faster than light, across a universe to relieve another sorely tried civilization.

Knowing their cause was lost, hopeless in the knowledge that nothing known to them could battle that enormous force concentrated in one ship, the *Thought*, the Thessians had but one aim now, to do all the damage in their power before leaving.

Already their tremendous, unarmed and unarmored transports were departing with their hundreds of thousands from that base system for the far-off Island of Space from which they had come. Their battlefleets were engaged in destroying all the cities of the allies, and those other helpless races of our system that they could. Those other inhabited worlds, many of which were completely wiped out because Arcot had no knowledge of them, were relieved only when the general call for retreat to protect the mother planet was sent out.

But Sirius was looming enormous before them. And its planets, heavily defended now by the combined Sirian, Terrestrial and Venerian fleets and great ray screens as well as a few matter-bomb stations, were suffering losses none the less. For the old Sixth of Negra, the Third here, had fallen. Slipping in on the night side of the planet, all power off, and so sending forth no warning impulses till it actually fell through the ray screen, a small fleet of scouts had entered. Falling still under simple gravity, they had been missed by the rays till they had fallen to so small a distance, that no humans or men of our allied systems could have stopped, but only their enormous iron boned strength permitted them to resist the acceleration they used to avert collision with the planet. Then scattering swiftly, they had blasted the great protective screen stations by attacking on the sides, where the ray screen projectors were not mounted. Designed to protect above, they had no side armor, and the Sixth was opened to attack.

Two and one-half billion people lost their lives painlessly and instantaneously as tremendous diffused moleculars played on the revolving planet.

Arcot arrived soon after this catastrophe. The Thessians left almost immediately, after the loss of three hundred or more ships. One hundred and fifty wrecks were found. The rest were so blasted by the forces which attacked them, that no traces could be found, and no count made.

But as those ships fled back to their base, Arcot, with the wonderfully delicate mental control of his ship, was able to watch them, and follow them; for, invisible under normal conditions, by twisting space in the same manner that they did he was able to see them flee, and follow.

Light year after light year they raced toward the distant base. They reached it in two hours, and Arcot saw them from a distance sink to the various worlds. There were twelve gigantic worlds, each far larger than Jupiter of Sol, and larger than Stwall of Talso's sun, Renl.

"I think," said Arcot as he stopped the ship at a third of a light year, "that we had best destroy those planets. We may kill many men, and innocent non-combatants, but they have killed many of our races, and it is necessary. There are, no doubt, other worlds of this Universe here that we do not know of that have felt the vengeance of Thett, and if we can cause such trouble to them by destroying these worlds, and putting the fear of our attacking their mother world into them, they will call off those other fleets. I could have been invisible to Thett's ships as we followed them here, and for the greater part of the way I was, for I was sufficiently out of their time-rate, so that they were visible only by the short ultra-violet, which would have put in their infra-red, and, no photo-electric cell will work on quanta of such low energy. When at last I was sure of the sun for which they were heading, I let them see us, and they know we are aware of their base, and that we can follow them.

"I will destroy one of these worlds, and follow a fleet as it starts for their home nebula. Gradually, as they run, I will fade into invisibility, and they will not know that I have dropped back here to complete the work, but will think I am still following. Probably they will run to some other nebula in an effort to throw me off, but they will most certainly send back a ship to call the fleets here to the defense of Thett.

"I think that is the best plan. Do you agree?"

"Arcot," asked Morey slowly, "if this race attempts to settle another Universe, what would that indicate of their own?"

"Hmmm — that it was either populated by their own race or that another race held the parts they did not, and that the other race was stronger," replied Arcot. "The thought idea in their minds has always been a single world, single solar system as their home, however."

"And single solar systems cannot originate in this Space," replied Morey, referring to the fact that in the primeval gas from which all matter in this Universe and all others came, no condensation of mass less than thousands of millions of times that of a sun could form and continue.

"We can only investigate — and hope that they do not inhabit the whole system, for I am determined that, unpleasant as the idea may be, there is one race that we cannot afford to have visiting us, and it is going to be permanently restrained in one way or another. I will first have a conference with their leaders and if they will not be peaceful — the *Thought* can destroy or make a Universe! But I think that a second race holds part of that Universe, for several times we have read in their minds the thought of the 'Mighty Warless Ones of Venone.'"

"And how do you plan to destroy so large a planet as these are?" asked Morey, indicating the telectroscope screen.

"Watch and see!" said Arcot.

They shot suddenly toward the distant sun, and as it expanded, planets came into view. Moving ever slower on the time control, Arcot drove the ship toward a gigantic planet at a distance of approximately 300,000,000 miles from its primary, the sun of this system.

Arcot fell into step with the planet as it moved about in its orbit, and watched the speed indicator carefully.

"What's the orbital speed, Morey?" asked Arcot.

"About twelve and a half miles per second," replied the somewhat mystified Morey.

"Excellent, my dear Watson," replied Arcot. "And now does my dear friend know the average molecular velocity of ordinary air?"

"Why, about one-third of a mile a second, average."

"And if that planet as a whole should stop moving, and the individual molecules be given the entire energy, what would their average velocity be? And what temperature would that represent?" asked Arcot.

"Good — Why, they would have to have the same kinetic energy as individuals as they now have as a whole, and that would be an average molecular velocity in random motion of 12.5 miles a second — giving about — about — about — twelve thousand degrees centigrade!" exclaimed Morey in surprise. "That would put it in the far blue-white region!"

"Perfect. Now watch." Arcot donned the headpiece he had removed, and once more took charge. He was very far from the planet, as distances go, and they could not see his ship. But he wanted to be seen. So he moved closer, and hung off to the sunward side of the planet, then moved to the night side, but stayed in the light. In seconds, a battlefleet was out attempting to destroy him.

Surrounding the ship with a wall of artificial matter, lest they annoy him, he set to work.

Directly in the orbit of the planet, a faint mistiness appeared, and rapidly solidified to a titanic cup, directly in the path of the planet.

Arcot was pouring energy into the making of that matter at such a rate that space was twisted now about them. The meter before them, which had not registered previously, was registering now, and had moved over to three. Three sols — and was still climbing. It stopped when ten were reached. Ten times the energy of our sun was pouring into that condensation, and it solidified quickly.

The Thessians had seen the danger now. It was less than ten minutes away from their planet, and now great numbers of ships of all sorts started up from the planet, swarming out like rats from a sinking vessel.

Majestically the great world moved on in its orbit toward the thin wall of infinite strength and infinite toughness. Already Thessian battleships were tearing at that wall with rays of all types, and the wall sputtered back little gouts of light, and remained. The meters on the *Thought* were no longer registering. The wall was built, and now Arcot had all the giant power of the ship holding it there. Any attempt to move it or destroy it, and all the energy of the Universe would rush to its defense!

The atmosphere of the planet reached the wall. Instantly, as the pressure of that enormous mass of air touched it, the wall fought, and burst into a blaze of energy. It was fighting now, and the meter that measured sun-powers ran steadily, swiftly up the scale. But the men were not watching the meter; they were watching the awesome sight of Man stopping a world in its course! Turning a world from its path!

But the meter climbed suddenly, and the world was suddenly a tremendous blaze of light. The solid rock had struck the giant cup, 110,000 miles in diameter. It was silent, as a world pitted its enormous kinetic energy against the combined forces of a universe. Soundless — and as hopeless. Its strength was nothing, its energy pitted unnoticed against the energy of five hundred thousand million suns — as vain as those futile attempts of the Thessian battleships on the invulnerable walls of the *Thought*.

What use is there to attempt description of that scene as 2,500,000,000,000,000,000,000 tons of rock and metal and matter crashed against a wall of energy, immovable and inconceivable. The planet crumpled, and split wide. A thousand pieces, and suddenly there was a further mistiness about it, and the whole enormous mass, seeming but a toy, as it was from this distance in space, and as it was in this ship, was enclosed in that same, immovable, unalterable wall of energy.

The ship was as quiet and noiseless, as without indication of strain as when it hummed its way through empty space. But the planet crumpled and twirled, and great seas of energy flashed about it.

The world, seeming tiny, was dashed helpless against a wall that stopped it, but the wall flared into equal and opposite energy, so that matter was raised not to the twelve thousand Morey had estimated but nearer twenty-four thousand degrees. It was over in less than half an hour, and a broken, misshapen mass of blue incandescence floated in space. It would fall now, toward the sun, and it would, because it was motionless and the sun moved, take an eccentric orbit about that sun. Eventually, perhaps, it would wipe out the four inferior planets, or perhaps it would be broken as it came within the Roches limit of that sun. But the planet was now a miniature sun, and not so very small, at that.

And from every planet of the system was pouring an assorted stream of ships, great and small, and they all set panic-stricken across the void in the same direction. They had seen the power of the *Thought*, and did not contest any longer its right to this system.

CHAPTER XXII

THETT

Through the utter void of intergalactic space sped a tiny shell, a wee mite of a ship. Scarcely twenty feet long, it was one single power plant. The man who sat alone in it, as it tore through the void at the maximum speed that even its tiny mass was capable of, when every last twist possible had been given to the distorted time fields, watched a far, far galaxy ahead that seemed unchanging.

Hours, days sped by, and he did not move from his position in the ship. But the ship had crossed the great gulf, and was speeding through the galaxy now. He was near the end. At a reckless speed, he sat motionless before the controls, save for slight movements of supple fingers that directed the ship at a mad pace about some gigantic sun and its family of planets. Suns flashed, grew to discs, and were left behind in the briefest instant.

The ship slowed, the terrific pace it had been holding fell, and dull whine of overworked generators fell to a contented hum. A star was looming, expanding before it. The great sun glowed the characteristic red of a giant as the ship slowed to less than a light-speed, and turned toward a gigantic planet that circled the red sun. The planet was very close to 50,000 miles in diameter, and it revolved at a distance of four and one half billions of miles from the surface of its sun, which made the distance to the center of the titanic primary four billion, eight hundred million miles, in round figures, for the sun's diameter was close to six hundred and fifty million miles! Greater even than Antares, whose diameter is close to four hundred million miles, was this star of another universe, and even from the billions of miles of distance that its planet revolved, the disc was enormous, a titanic disc of dull red flame. But so low was its surface temperature, that even that enormous disc did not overheat the giant planet.

The planet's atmosphere stretched out tens of thousands of miles into space, and under the enormous gravitational accelera-tion of the tremendous mass of that planet, it was near the surface a blanket dense as water. There was no temperature change upon it, though its night was one hundred hours long, and its day the same. The centrifugal force of the rapid rotation of this enormous body had flattened it when still liquid till it seemed now more of the shape of a pumpkin than of an orange. It was really a double planet, for its satellite was a world of one hundred thousand miles diameter, yet smaller in comparison to its giant primary than is Luna in comparison to Earth. It revolved at a distance of five million miles from its primary's center, and it, too, was swarming with its people.

But the racing ship sped directly toward the great planet, and shrieked its way down through the atmosphere, till its outer shell was radiating far in the violet.

Straight it flew to where a gigantic city sprawled in the heaped, somber masonry, but in some order yet, for on closer inspection the appearance of interlaced circles came over the edge of the giant cities. Ray screens were circular and the city was protected by dozens of stations.

The scout was going well under the speed of light now, and a message, imperative and commanding, sped ahead of him. Half a dozen patrol boats flashed up, and fell in beside him, and with him raced to a gigantic building that reared its somber head from the center of the city.

Under a white sky they proceeded to it, and landed on its roof. From the little machine the single man came out. Using the webbed hands and feet that had led the Allied scientists to think them an aquatic race, he swam upward, and through the water-dense atmosphere of the planet toward the door.

Trees overtopped the building, for it had but four stories, above ground, though it was the tallest in the city. The trees, like seaweed, floated most of their enormous weight in the dense air, but the buildings under the gravitational acceleration, which was more than one hundred times Earth's gravity, could not be built very high ere they crumple under their own weight. Though one of these men weighed approximately two hundred pounds on Earth, for all their short stature, on this planet their weight was more than ten tons! Only the enormously dense atmosphere permitted them to move.

And such an atmosphere! At a temperature of almost exactly 360 degrees centigrade, there was no liquid water on the planet, naturally. At that temperature water cannot be a liquid, no matter what the pressure, and it was a gas. In their own bodies there was liquid water, but only because they lived on heat, their muscles absorbed their energy for work from the heat of the air. They carried in their own muscles refrigeration, and, with that aid, were able to keep liquid water for their life processes. With death, the water evaporated. Almost the entire atmosphere was made up of oxygen, with but a trace of nitrogen, and some amount of carbon dioxide.

Here their enormous strength was not needed, as Arcot had supposed, to move their own bodies, but to enable them to perform the ordinary tasks of life. The mere act of lifting a thing weighing perhaps ten pounds on Earth, here required a lifting force of more than half a ton! No wonder enormous strength had been developed! Such things as a man might carry with him, perhaps a ray pistol, would weigh half a ton; his money would weigh near to a hundred pounds!

But — there were no guns on this world. A man could throw a stone perhaps a short distance, but when a gravitational acceleration of more than a half a mile per second acted on it, and it was hurled through an atmosphere dense as water — what chance was there for a long range?

But these little men of enormous strength did not know other schemes of existence, save in the abstract, and as things of comical peculiarity. To them life on a planet like Earth was as life to a terrestrian on a planetoid such as Ceres, Juno or Eros would have seemed. Even on Thettsost, the satellite planet of Thett, life was strange, and they used lux roofs over their cities, though their weight there was four tons!

As the scout swam through the dense atmosphere of his world toward the entrance way to the building, guards stopped him, and examined his credentials. Then he was led through long halls, and down a shaft ten stories below the planet's surface, to where a great table occupied a part of a low ceilinged, wide room. This room was shielded, interference screens of all known kinds lined the hollow walls, no rays could reach through it to the men within. The guard changed, and new men examined the scout's credentials, and he was led still deeper into the bowels of the planet. Once more the guard changed, and he entered a room guarded not by single shields but by triple, and walled with six foot relux, and ceiled with the same strong material. But here, under the enormous gravity, even its great strength required aid in the form of pillars.

A giant of his race sat before a low table. The table ran half the length of the room, and beside it sat four other men. But there were places for more than two dozen.

"A scout from the colony? What news?" demanded the leader. His voice was a growl, deep and throaty.

"Oh mighty Sthanto, I bring news of resistance. We waited too long, in our explorations, and those men of World 3769-8482730-3 have learned too much. We were wrong. They had found the secret of exceeding the speed of light, and can travel through space fully as rapidly as we can, and now, since by some means we cannot fathom, they have learned to combine both our own system and theirs, they have one enormous engine of destruction that travels across their huge universe in less time than it takes us to travel across a planetary system.

"Our cause is lost, which is by far the least of our troubles. Thett is in danger. We cannot hope to combat that ship."

"Thalt — what means have we. Can we not better them?" demanded Sthanto of his chief scientist.

"Great Sthanto, we know that such a substance can be made when pressure can be brought to bear on cosmic rays under the influence of field 24-7649-321, but that field cannot be produced, because no sufficient concentration of energy is available. Energy cannot be released rapidly enough to replace the losses when the field is developing. The fact that they have that material indicates their possession of an unguessed and terrific energy source. I would have said that there was no energy greater than the energy of matter, but we know the properties of this material and that the triple ray which has at last been perfected, can be produced providing your order for all energy sources is given, will release its energy at a speed comparable to the rate of energy relux in a twin ray, but that the release takes place only in the path of the ray."

"What more, Scout?" asked Sthanto smoothly.

"The ship first appeared in connection with our general attack on world 3769-8482730-3. The attack was near success, their screens were already failing. They have devised a new and very ionized layer as a conductor. It was exceedingly difficult to break, and since their sun had been similarly screened, we could not throw masses of that matter upon them.

"In another sthan of time, we would have destroyed their world. Then the ship appeared. It has molecular rays, magnetic beams and cosmic rays, and a fourth weapon we know nothing of. It has molecular screens, we suspect, but has not had occasion to use them.

"Our heaviest molecular screens flash under their molecular rays. Ordinary screens fall instantly without momentary defense. The ray power is incalculable.

"Their magnetic beams are used in conjunction with cosmics. The action of the two causes the relux to induce current, and due to reaction of currents on the magnetic field —"

"And the resistance due to the relux, the relux is first heated to incandescence and then the ship opens out as the air pressure bends the magnetically softened relux?" finished Thalt.

"No, the effect is even more terrific. It explodes into powder," replied the scout.

"And what happens to worlds that the magnetic ray touches?" inquired the scientist.

"A corner of it touched the world we fought over, and the world shook," replied the colonist.

"And the last weapon?" asked Sthanto, his voice soft now.

"It seems a ghost. It is a mistiness that comes into existence like a cloud, and what it touches is crushed, what it rams is shattered. It surrounds the great ship, and machines crashing into it at a speed of more than six times that of light are completely destroyed, without in the slightest injuring the shield.

"Then — what caused my departure from the colony — it showed once more its unutterable power. The mistiness formed in the path of our colonial world, number 3769-1-5, and the planet swept against that wall of mistiness, and was shattered, and turned in less than five sthan to a ball of blue-white fire. The wall stopped the planet in its motion. We could not fight that machine, and we left the worlds. The others are coming," finished the scout.

The ruler turned his slightly smiling face to the commander of his armies, who sat beside him.

"Give orders," he said softly, almost gently, "that a triple ray station be set up under the direction of Thalt, and further notice that all power be made instantly available to it. Add that the colonists are returning defeated, and bringing danger at their heels. The triple ray will destroy each ship as it enters the system." His hand under the table pushed an invisible protuberance, and from the perfectly conducting relux floor to the equally perfectly conducting ceiling, and between four pillars grouped around the spot where the scout stood, terrific arcs suddenly came into being. They lasted for the thousandth part of a second, and when they suddenly died away, as swiftly as they had come, there was not even ash where the scout had been.

"Have you any suggestions, Thalt?" he asked of the scientist, his voice as soft as before.

"I quite agree with your conduct so far, but the future conduct you had planned is quite unsatisfactory," replied the scientist. The ruler sat motionless in his great seat, staring fixedly at the scientist. "I think it is time I take your place, therefore." The place where the ruler had been was suddenly seen as through a dark cloud, then the cloud was gone, and with it the king, only his relux chair, and the bits of lux or relux that had been about his garments remained.

"He was a fool," said the scientist softly, as he rose, "to plan on removing his scientist. Are there any who object to my succession?"

"No one objects," said Faslar, the ex-king's Prime Minister and councilor.

"Then I think, Phantal, Commander of planetary forces, that you had best see Ranstud, my assistant, and follow out the plan outlined by my predecessor. And you Tastal, Commander of Fleets, had best bring your fleets near the planets for protection. Go."

"May I suggest, mighty Thalt," said Faslar after the others had left, "that my knowledge will be exceedingly useful to you. You have two commanders, neither of whom loves you, and neither of whom is highly capable. The family of Thadstil would be glad to learn who removed that honored gentleman, and the family of Datstir would gladly support him who brought the remover of their head to them.

"This would remove two unwelcome menaces, and open places for such as Ranstud and your son Warrtil.

"And," he said hastily as he saw a slight shift in Thalt's eyes, "I might say further that the bereaved ones of Parthel would find great interest in certain of my papers, which are only protected by my personal constant watchfulness."

"Ah, so? And what of Kelston Faln, Faslar?" smiled the new Sthanta.

Thalt's hand relaxed and they started a conversation and discussion on means of defense.

CHAPTER XXIII

VENONE

Up from Earth, out of its clear blue sky, and into the glare and dark of space and near a sun the ship soared. They had been holding it motionless over New York, and now as it rose, hundreds of tiny craft, and a few large excursion ships followed it until it was out of Earth's atmosphere. Then — it was gone. Gone across space, racing toward that far Universe at a speed no other thing could equal. In minutes the great disc of the Universe had taken form behind them, as they took their route photographs to find their way back to Earth after the battle, if still they could come.

Then into the stillness of the Intergalactic spaces.

"This will be our first opportunity to test the full speed of this ship. We have never tried its velocity, and we should measure it now. Take a sight on the diameter of the Island, as seen from here, Morey. Then we will travel ten seconds, and look again."

Half a million light years from the center of the Island now, the great disc spread out over the vast space behind them, apparently the size of a dinner plate at about thirty inches distance, it was more than two hundred and fifty thousand light years across. Checking carefully, Morey read their distance as just shy of five hundred thousand light years.

"Hold on — here we go," called Arcot. Space was suddenly black, and beside them ran the twin ghost ships that follow always when space is closed to the smallest compass, for light leaving, goes around a space whose radius is measured in miles, instead of light centuries and returns. There was no sound, no slightest vibration, only Torlos' iron bones felt a slight shock as the inconceivable currents flowed into the gigantic space distortion coil from the storage fields, their shielded magnetic flux leaking by in some slight degree.

For ten seconds that seemed minutes Arcot held the ship on the course under the maximum combined powers of space distortion and time field distortion. Then he released both simultaneously.

The velvet black of space was about them as before, but now the disc of the Nebula was tiny behind them! So tiny was it, that these men, who knew its magnitude, gasped in sudden wonder. None of them had been able to conceive of such a velocity as this ship had shown! In seconds, Morey announced a moment later, they had traveled *one million, one hundred thousand light years*! Their velocity was six hundred and sixty quadrillion miles per second!

"Then it will take us only a little over one thousand seconds to travel the hundred and fifty million light years, at 110,000 light years per second — that's about the radius of our galaxy, isn't it!" exclaimed Wade.

They started on now, and one thousand and ten seconds, or a little more than eighteen minutes later, they stopped again. So far behind them now as to be almost lost in the far scattered universes, lay their own Island, and carefully they photographed the Universe that now lay less than twenty million light years ahead. Still, it was further, even after crossing this enormous gulf, than are many of those nebulae we see from Earth, many of which lie within that distance. They must proceed cautiously now, for they did not know the exact distance to the Nebula. Carefully, running forward in jumps of five million light years, forty-five second drives, they worked nearer.

Then finally they entered the Island, and drove toward the denser center.

"Good Lord, Arcot, look at those suns!" exclaimed Morey in amazement. For the first time they were seeing the suns of this system at a range that permitted observation, and Arcot had stopped to observe. The first one they had chosen had been a blue-white giant of enormous mass, nearly one hundred and fifty times as heavy as our own sun, and all the enormous surface was radiating power into space at a rate of nearly thirty thousand horsepower per square inch! No planets circled it, however, in its journey through space.

"I've been noticing the number of giants here. Look around."

The *Thought* moved on, on to other suns. They must find one that was inhabited.

They stopped at last near a great orange giant, and examined it. It had indeed planets, and as Arcot watched, he saw in the telectroscope a line of gigantic freighters rise from the world, and whisk off to nothingness as they exceeded the speed of light! Instantly he started the *Thought* searching in time fields for the freighters. He found them, and followed them as they raced across the void. He knew he was visible to them, and as he suspected, they soon stopped, slowing down and signaling to him.

"Morey — take the *Thought*. I'm going to visit them in the *Banderlog* as I think we shall name the tender," called Arcot, stripping off the headset, and leaving the control seat. The other fleet of ships was now less than a hundred thousand miles away, clearly visible in the telectroscope. They were still signaling, and Arcot had set an automatic signaling device flashing an enormously powerful searchlight toward them in a succession of dots and dashes, an obvious signal, though also, obviously unintelligible to those others.

"Is it safe, Arcot?" asked Torlos anxiously. To approach those enormous ships in the relatively tiny *Banderlog* seemed unwise.

"Far safer than they'll believe. Remember, only the *Thought* could stand up against such weapons as even the *Banderlog* carries, run as they are by cosmic energy," replied Arcot, diving down toward the little tender.

In a moment it was out through the lock, and sped away from them like a bullet, reaching the distant stranger fleet in less than ten seconds.

"They are communicating by thought!" announced Zezdon Afthen presently. "But I cannot understand them, for the impulses are too weak to be intelligently received."

For nearly an hour the *Banderlog* hung beside the fleet, then it turned about, and raced once more to the *Thought*. Inside the lock, and a moment later Arcot appeared again on the threshold of the door. He looked immensely relieved.

"Well, I have some good news," he said and smiled, sitting down. "Follow that bunch, Morey, and I'll tell you about it. Set it and she'll hold nicely. We have a long way to go, and those are slow freighters, accompanied by one Cruiser.

"Those men," he began, "are men of Venone. You remember Thett's records said something of the Mighty Warless Ones of Venone? Those are they. They inhabit most of this universe, leaving the Thessians but four planets of a minor sun, way off in one corner. It seems the Thessians are their undesirable exiles, those who have, from generation to generation, been either forced to go there, or who wanted to go there.

"They did not like the easier and more effective method of disposing of undesirables, the instantaneous death chamber they now use. Thett was their prison world. No one ever returned and his family could go with him if they desired, but if they did not, they were carefully watched for outcroppings of undesirable traits — murder, crime of any sort, any habitual tendency to injustice.

"About six hundred years ago of our time, Thett revolted. There were scientists there, and their scientists had discovered a thing that they had been seeking for generations — the Twin-ray. I don't know what it is, and the Venonians don't either. It is the ray that destroys relux and lux, however, and can be carried only on a machine the size of their forts, due to some limitations. Just what those limitations are the Venonians don't know. Other than that ray they had no new weapons.

"But it was enough. Their guard ships which had circled the worlds of the prison system, Antseck, were suddenly destroyed, so suddenly that Venone received no word of it till a consignment ship, bringing prisoners, discovered their absence. The consignment ship returned without landing. Thett was now independent. But they were bound to their system, for although they had the molecular ships, they had never been permitted to have time apparatus, nor to see it, nor was any one who knew its principles ever consigned there. The result was that they were as isolated as ever.

"This was for two centuries. Two centuries later it was worked out by one of their scientists, and the Warless Ones had a War of defense. Their small fleet of cruisers, designed for rescue work and for clearing space lanes of wrecks and asteroids, was destroyed instantly, their world was protected only by the ray screen, which the Thessians did not have, and by the fact that they could build more cruisers. In less than a year Thett was defeated, and beaten back to her world, though Venone could not overcome Thett, now, for around their planets they had so many forts projecting the deadly rays, that no ship could approach.

"Then Thett learned how to make the screen, and came again. Venone had planetoid stations, that projected molecular rays of an intensity I wonder at, with their system of projecting. It seems these people have force-power feeds that operate through space, by which an entire solar system can tie in for power, and they fed these stations in that way. Lord only knows what tubes they had, but the Thessians couldn't get the power to fight.

"They've been let alone since then, they did not know why. I told them what their dear friends had been doing in that time, and the Venonians were immensely surprised, and very evidently sorry. They begged my pardon for letting loose such a menace, quite sincerely feeling that it was their fault. They offered any help they could give, and I told them that a chart of this system would be of the greatest use. They are going now to Venone, and we are to go with them, and see what they have to offer. Also, they want a demonstration of this 'remarkable ship that can defeat whole fleets of Thessians, and destroy or make planets at will,'" concluded Arcot.

"I do not in the least blame them for wanting to see this ship in operation, Arcot, but they are, very evidently, a much older race than yours," said Torlos, his thoughts coming clear and sharp, as those of a man who has thought over what he says carefully. "Are you not running danger that their minds may be more powerful than yours, that this story they have told you is but a ruse to get this ship on their world where thousand, millions can concentrate their will against you and capture the ship by mind where they cannot capture it by force?"

"That," agreed Arcot, "is where 'the rub' comes in as an ancient poet of Earth put it. I don't know and I did not have a chance to see. Wherefore I am about to do some work. Let me have the controls, Morey, will you?"

Arcot made a new ship. It was made entirely, perforce, of cosmium, lux and relux, for those were the only forms of matter he could create in space permanently from energy. It was equipped with gravity drive, and time distortion speed apparatus, and his far better trained mind finished this smaller ship with his titanic tools in less than the two days that it took them to reach Venone. In the meantime, the Venonian cruiser had drawn close, and watched in amazement as the ship was fashioned from the energy of space, became a thing of glistening matter, materializing from the absolute void of space, and forming under titanic tools such as the commander could not visualize.

Now, this move was partly the reason for this construction, for while the Venonian was busy, absorbed in watching the miraculous construction, his mind was not shielded, and it was open for observation of two such wonderfully trained minds as those of Zezdon Afthen and Zezdon Inthel. With their instruments and wonderfully developed mind-science, aided at times by Morey's less skillful, but more powerful mind of his older race, and powerful too, both because of long concentration and training, and because of his individual inheritance, they examined the minds of many of the officers of the ship without their awareness.

As a final test, Arcot, having finished the ship, suggested that the Venonian officer and one of the men of his ship have a trial of mental powers.

Zezdon Afthen tried first, and between the two ships, racing along side by side at a speed unthinkable, the two men struggled with those forces of will.

Quickly Zezdon Afthen told Arcot what he had learned.

The sun of Venone was close, now, and Arcot prepared to use

as he intended the little space machine he had made. Morey took it, and went away from the *Thought* flying on its time field. The ship had been stocked with lead fuel for its matter-burning generators from the supply that had been brought on the *Thought* for emergencies, and the air had come from the *Thought*'s great tanks. Morey was going to Venone ahead of the *Thought* to scout — "to see many of the important men of Venone and find out from them what I can of the relationship between Venone and Thett."

Hours later Morey returned with a favorable report. He had seen many of the important men of Venone, and conversed with them mentally from the safety of his ship, where the specially installed gravity apparatus had protected him and the ship against the enormous gravity of this gigantic world. He did not describe Venone; he wanted them to see it as he had first seen it.

So the little ship, which had served its purpose now, was destroyed, nearly a light year from Venone, and left a crushed wreck when two plates of artificial matter had closed upon it, destroying the apparatus, lest some unwelcome finder use it. There was little about it, the gravity apparatus alone perhaps, that might have been of use to Thett, and Thett already had the ray — but why take needless risk?

Then once more they were racing toward Venone. Soon the giant star of which it was a planet loomed enormous. Then, at Morey's direction, they swung, and before them loomed a planet. Large as Thett, near a half million miles in diameter, its mass was very closely equal to that of our sun. Yet it was but the burned-out sweepings of the outermost photospheric layers of this giant sun, and the radioactive atoms that made a sun active were not here; it was a cold planet. But its density was far, far higher than that of our sun, for our sun is but slightly denser than ordinary sea water. This world was dense as copper, for with the deeper sweepings of the tidal strains that had formed it, more of the heavier atoms had gone into its making, and its core was denser than that of Earth.

About it swept two gigantic satellite Worlds, each larger than Jupiter, but satellites of a satellite here! And Venone itself was inhabited by countless millions, yet their low, green tile and metal cities were invisible in the aspect of rolling lands with tiny hillocks, dwarfed by gigantic bulbous trees that floated their enormous weight in the water-dense atmosphere.

Here, too, there were no seas, for the temperature was above the critical temperature of water, and only in the self-cooling bodies of these men and in the trees which similarly cooled themselves, could there be liquid.

The sun of the world was another of the giant red stars, close to three hundred and fifty times the mass of our sun. It was circled by but three giant planets. Its enormous disc was almost invisible from the surface of the world as the *Thought* sank slowly through fifteen thousand miles of air, due to the screening effect on light passing through so much air. Earth could have rested on this planet and not extended beyond its atmosphere! Had Earth been situated at this planet's center, the Moon could have revolved about it, and would not have been beyond the planet's surface!

In silent wonder the terrestrians watched the titanic world as they sank, and their friends looked on amazed, comprehending even less of the significance of what they saw. Already within the titanic gravitational field, they could see that indescribable effects were being produced on them, and on the ship. Arcot alone could know the enormous gravitation, and his accelerometer told him now that he was subject to a gravitational acceleration of three thousand four hundred and eighty-seven feet per second, or almost exactly one hundred and nine times Earth's pull.

"The *Thought* weighs one billion, two hundred and six million, five hundred thousand tons, with tender, on Earth. Here it weighs approximately one hundred and twenty-one billion tons," said Arcot softly.

"Can you set it down? It may crush under this load if the gravity drive isn't supporting it," asked Torlos anxiously.

"Eight inches cosmium, and everything else supported by cosmium. I made this thing to stand any conceivable strain. Watch — if the planet's surface will take the load," replied Arcot.

They were still sinking, and now a number of small marvelously streamlined ships were clustered around the slowly settling giant. In a few moments more people, hundreds, thousands of men were flying through the air up to the ship.

A cruiser had appeared, and was very evidently intent on leading them somewhere, and Arcot followed it as it streaked through the dense air. "No wonder they streamline," he muttered as he saw the enormous force it took to drive the gigantic ship through this air. The air pressure outside their ship now was so great, that the sheer crushing effect of the air pressure alone was enormous. The pressure was well over nine tons to the square inch, on the surface of that enormous ship!

They landed approximately fifty miles from a large city which was the capital. The land seemed absolutely level, and the horizon faded off in distance in an atmosphere absolutely clear. There was no dust in the air at their height of nearly three hundred feet, for dust was too heavy on this world. There were no clouds. The mountains of this enormous world were not large, could not be large, for their sheer weight would tear them down, but what mountains there were were jagged, tortured rock, exceedingly sharp in outline.

"No rain — no temperature change to break them down," said Wade looking at them. "The zone of fracture can't be deep here."

"What, Wade, is the zone of fracture?" asked Torles.

"Rock has weight. Any substance, no matter how brittle, will flow if sufficient pressure is brought to bear from all sides. A thing which can flow will not break or fracture. You can't imagine the pressure to which the rock three hundred feet down is subject to. There is the enormous mass of atmosphere, the tremendous mass of rock above, and all forced down by this gravitation. By the time you get down half a mile, the rock is under such an inconceivably great pressure that it will flow like mud. The rock there cannot break; it merely flows under pressure. Above, the rock can break, instead of flowing. That is the zone of fracture. On Earth the zone of fracture is ten miles deep. Here it must be of the order of only five hundred feet! And the planetary blocks that made a planet's surface float on the zone of flowage — they determine the zone of fracture."

The gigantic ship had been sinking, and now, suddenly it gave a very unexpected demonstration of Wade's words. It had landed, and Arcot shut off the power. There was a roaring, and the giant ship trembled, rocked, and rolled along a bit. Instantly Arcot drove it into the air.

"Whoa — can't do it. The ship will stand it, and won't bend under the load — but the planet won't. We caused a Venone-quake. One of those planetary blocks Wade was talking about slipped under the added strain."

Quickly Wade explained that all the planetary blocks were floating, truly floating, and in equilibrium just as a boat must be. The added load had been sufficiently great, so that, with an already extant overload on this particular planetary block, this "boat" had sunk a bit further into the flowage zone, till it was once more at rest and balanced.

"They wish us to come out that they may see us, strangers and friends from another Island," interrupted Zezdon Afthen.

"Tell them they'd have to scrape us up off the ground, if we attempted it. We come from a world where we weigh about as much as a pebble here," said Wade, grinning at the thought of terrestrians trying to walk on this world.

"Don't — tell them we'll be right out," said Arcot sharply. "All of us."

Morey and the others all stared at Arcot in amazement. It was utterly impossible!

But Zezdon Afthen did as Arcot had asked. Almost immediately, another Morey stepped out of the airlock wearing what was obviously a pressure suit. Behind him came another Wade, Torlos, Stel Felso Theu, and indeed all the members of their party save Arcot himself! The Galactians stared in wonder — then comprehended and laughed together. Arcot had sent artificial matter images of them all!

Their images stepped out, and the Venonian crowd which had collected, stared in wonder at the giants, looming twice their height above them.

"You see not us, but images of us. We cannot withstand your gravity nor your air pressure, save in the protection of our ship. But these images are true images of us."

For some time then they communicated, and finally Arcot agreed to give a demonstration of their power. At the suggestion of the cruiser commander who had seen the construction of a spaceship from the emptiness of space, Arcot rapidly constructed a small, very simple, molecular drive machine of pure cosmium, making it entirely from energy. It required but minutes, and the Venonians stared in wonder as Arcot's unbelievable tools created the machine before their eyes. The completed ship Arcot gave to an official of the city who had appeared. The Venonian looked at the thing skeptically, and half expecting it to vanish like the tools that made it, gingerly entered the port. Powered as it was by lead burning cosmic ray generators, the lead alone having been made by transmutation of natural matter, it was powerful, and speedy. The official entered it, and finding it still existing, tried it out. Much to his amazement it flew, and operated perfectly.

Nearly ten hours Arcot and his friends stayed at Venone, and before they left, the Venonians, for all their vast differences of structure, had proven themselves true, kindly honest men, and a race that our Alliance has since found every reason to respect and honor. Our commerce with them, though carried on under difficulties, is none the less a bond of genuine friendship.

CHAPTER XXIV

THETT PREPARES

Streaking through the void toward Thett was again a tiny scout ship. It carried but a single man, and with all the power of the machine he was darting toward distant Thett, at a speed insanely reckless, but he knew that he must maintain such a speed if his mission were to be successful.

Again a tiny ship entered Thett's far-flung atmosphere, and slowed to less than a light speed, and sent its signal call ahead. In moments the patrol ship, less than three hundred miles away, had reached it, and together they streaked through the dense air in a screaming dive toward Shatnsoma, the capital city. It was directly beneath, and it was not long before they had reached the great palace grounds, and settled on the upper roof. Then the scout leaped out of his tiny craft, and dove for the door. Flashing his credentials, he dove down, and into the first shielded room. Here precious seconds were wasted while a check was made of the credentials the man carried, then he was sent through to the Council Room. And he, too, stood on that exact spot where the other scout, but a few weeks before, had stood — and vanished. Waiting, it seemed, were four councilors and the new Sthanto, Thalt.

"What news, Scout?" asked the Sthanto.

"They have arrived in the Universe to Venone, and gone to the planet Venone. They were on the planet when I left. None of our scouts were able to approach the place, as there were innumerable Venonian watchers who would have recognized our deeper skin-color, and destroyed us. Two scouts were rayed, though the Galactians did not see this. Finally we captured two Venonians who had seen it, and attempted to force the information we needed from them. A young man and his chosen mate.

"The man would tell nothing, and we were hurried. So we turned to the girl. These accursed Venonians are courageous for all their pacifism. We were hurried, and yet it was long before we forced her to tell what we needed to know so vitally. She had been one of the notetakers for the Venonian government. We got most of their conversation, but she died of burns before she finished.

"The Galactians know nothing of the twin-ray beyond its action, and that it is an electro-magnetic phenomenon, though they have been able to distort it by using a sheet of pure energy. But their walls are impregnable to it, and their power of creating matter from the pure energy of space, as we saw from a distance, would enable them to easily defeat it, were it not that the twin-ray passes through matter without harming it. Any ray which will destroy matter of the natural electrical types, will be stopped.

"The girl was damnably clever, for she gave us only the things we already knew, and but few new facts; knowing that she would inevitably die soon, she talked — but it was empty talk. The one thing of import we have learned is that they burn no fuel, use no fuel of any sort but in some inconceivable manner get their energy from the radiations of the suns of space. This could not be great — but we know she told the truth, and we know their power is great. She told the truth, for we could determine when she lied, by mental action, of course.

"But more we could not learn. The man died without telling anything, merely cursing. He knew nothing anyway, as we already had determined," concluded the scout.

Silently the Sthanto sat in thought for some moments. Then he raised his head, and looked at the scout once more.

"You have done well. You secured some information of import, which was more than we had dared hope for. But you managed things poorly. The woman should not have died so soon. We can only guess.

"The radiation of the suns of space — hmmm —" Sthanto Thalt's brow wrinkled in thought. "The radiation of the *suns* of space. Were his power derived from the sun near which he is operating, he would not have said *suns*. It was more than one?"

"It was, oh Sthanto," replied the scout positively.

"His power is unreasonable. I doubt that he gave the true explanation. It may well have been that he did not trust the Venonians. I would not, for all their warless ways. But surely the suns of space give very little power at any given point at random. Else space would not be cold.

"But go, Scout, and you will be assigned a position in the fleet. The Colonial fleet, the remains of it, have arrived, and the colonists been removed. They failed. We will use their ships. You will be assigned." The scout left, and was indeed assigned to a ship of the colonists. The incoming colonial transports had been met at the outposts of the system, and rayed out of existence at once — failures, and bringing danger at their heels. Besides — there was no room for them on Thett without Thessians being crowded uncomfortably.

As their battleships arrived they were conducted to one of the satellites, and each man was "fumigated," lest he bring disease to the mother planet. Men entered, men apparently emerged. But they were different men.

"It seems," said the Sthanto softly, after the scout had left, "that we will have little difficulty, for they are, we know, vulnerable to the triple ray. And if we can but once destroy their driving units they will be helpless on our world. I doubt that wild tale of their using no fuel. Even if that be true they will be helpless with their power apparatus destroyed, and — if we miss the first time, we can seek it out, or drive them off!

"All of which is dependent on the fact that they attack at a point where we have a triple ray station to meet them. There are but three of these, actually, but I have had dummy stations, apparently identical with our other real stations, set up in many places.

"This gibberish we hear of creating matter — it is impossible, and surely unsuitable as a weapon. Their misty wall — that may be a force plane, but I know of no such possibility. The artificial substance though — why should any one make it? It but consumes energy, and once made is no more dangerous than ordinary matter, save that there is the possibility of creating it in dangerous position. Remember, we have heard already of the mental suggestions planes — mere force planes — *plus* a wonderfully developed power of suggestion. They do most of their damage by mental impression. Remember, we have heard already of the mental suggestions of horrible things that drove one fleet of the weak-minded colonists mad.

"And that, I think, we will use to protect ourselves. If we can, with the apparatus which you, my son, have developed, cause them to believe that all the other forts are equally dangerous, and that this one on Thett is the best point of attack — It will be easy. Can you do it?"

"I can, Oh Sthanto, if but a sufficient number of powerful minds may be brought to aid me," replied the youngest of the four councilmen.

"And you, Ranstud, are the stations ready?" asked the ruler.

"We are ready."

CHAPTER XXV

WITH GALAXIES IN THE BALANCE

The *Thought* arose from Venone after long hours, and at Arcot's suggestion, they assumed an orbit about the world, at a distance of two million miles, and all on board slept, save Torlos, the tireless molecular motion machine of flesh and iron. He acted as guard, and as he had slept but four days before, he explained there was really no reason for him to sleep as yet.

But the terrestrians would feel the greatest strain of the coming encounter, especially Arcot and Morey, for Morey was to help by repairing any damage done, by working from the control board of the *Banderlog*. The little tender had sufficient power to take care of any damage that Thett might inflict, they felt sure.

For they had not learned of the triple ray.

It was hours later that, rested and refreshed, they started for Thett. Following the great space-chart that they had been given by the Venonians, a series of blocks of clear lux metal, with tiny points of slowly disintegrating lux, such as had been used to illuminate the letters of the *Thought*'s name representing suns, the colors and relative intensity being shown. Then there was a more manageable guide in the form of photographs, marked for route by constellations formations as well, which would be their actual guide.

At the maximum speed of the time apparatus, for thus they could better follow the constellations, the *Thought* plunged along in the wake of the tiny scout ship that had already landed on Thett. And, hours later, they saw the giant red sun of Antseck, the star of Thett and its system.

"We're about there," said Arcot, a peculiar tenseness showing in his thoughts. "Shall we barge right in, or wait and investigate?"

"We'll have to chance it. Where is their main fort here?"

"From the direction, I should say it was to the left and ahead of our position," replied Zezdon Afthen.

The ship moved ahead, while about it the tremendous Thessian battlefleet buzzed like flies, thousands of ships now, and more coming with each second.

In a few moments the titanic ship had crossed a great plain, and came to a region of bare, rocky hills several hundred feet high. Set in those hills, surrounded by them, was a huge sphere, resting on the ground. As though by magic the Thessian fleet cleared away from the *Thought*. The last one had not left, when Arcot shot a terrific cosmic ray toward the sphere. It was relux, and he knew it, but he knew what would happen when that cosmic ray hit it. The solometer flickered and steadied at three as that inconceivable ray flashed out.

Instantly there was a terrific explosion. The soil exploded into hydrogen atoms, and expanded under heat that lashed it to more than a million degrees in the tiniest fraction of a second. The terrific recoil of the ray-pressure was taken by all space, for it was generated in space itself, but the direct pressure struck the planet, and that titanic planet reeled! A tremendous fissure opened, and the section that had been struck by the ray smashed its way suddenly far into the planet, and a geyser of fluid rock rolled over it, twenty miles deep in that world. The relux sphere had been struck by the ray, and had turned it, with the result that it was pushed doubly hard. The enormously thick relux strained and dented, then shot down as a whole, into the incandescent rock.

For miles the vaporized rock was boiling off. Then the fort sent out a ray, and that ray blasted the rock that had flowed over it as Arcot's titanic ray snapped out. In moments the fort was at the surface again — and a molecular hit it. The molecular did not have the energy the cosmic had carried, but it was a single concentrated beam of destruction ten feet across. It struck the fort — and the fort recoiled under its energy. The marvelous new tubes that ran its ray screen flashed instantly to a temperature inconceivable, and, so long as the elements embedded in the infusible relux remained the metals they were, those tubes could not fail. But they were being lashed by the energy of half a sun. The tubes failed. The elements heated to that enormous temperature when elements cannot exist — and broke to other elements that did not resist. The relux flashed into blinding iridescence —

And from the fort came a beam of pure silvery light. It struck the *Thought* just behind the bow, for the operator was aiming for the point where he knew the control room and pilot must be. But Arcot had designed the ship for mental control, which the enemy operator could not guess. The beam was a flat beam, perhaps an inch thick, but it fanned out to fifty feet width. And where it touched the *Thought*, there was a terrific explosion, and inconceivably violent energy lashed out as the cosmium instantaneously liberated its energy.

A hundred feet of the nose was torn off the ship, and the enormously dense air of Thett rushed in. But that beam had cut through the very edge of one of the ray projectors, or better, one of the ray feed apparatus. And the ray feed released it without control; it released all the energy it could suck in from space about it, as one single beam of cosmic energy, somewhat lower than the regular cosmics, and it flashed out in a beam as solid matter.

There was air about the ship, and the air instantly exploded into atoms of a different sort, threw off their electrons, and were raised to the temperature at which no atom can exist, and became protons and electrons. But so rapidly was that coil sucking energy from space that space tended to close in about it, and in enormous spurts the energy flooded out. It was directed almost straight up, and but one ship was caught in its beam. It was made of relux, but the relux was powdered under the inconceivable blow that countless quintillions of cosmic ray photons struck it. That ray was in fact, a solid mass of cosmium moving with the velocity of light. And it was headed for that satellite of Thett, which it would reach in a few hours time.

The *Thought*, due to the spatial strains of the wounded coil, was constantly rushing away to an almost infinite distance, as the ship approached that other space toward which the coil tended with its load, and rushing back, as the coil, reaching a spatial condition which supplied no energy, fell back. In a hundredth of a second it had reached equilibrium, and they were in a weirdly, terribly distorted space. But the triple-ray of the Thessians seemed to sheer off, and miss, no matter how it was directed. And it was painfully weak, for the coil sucked up the energy of whatsoever matter disintegrated in the neighborhood.

Then suddenly the performance was over. And they plunged into artificial space that was black and clean, and not a thing of wavering, struggling energies. Morey, from his control in the *Banderlog*, had succeeded in getting sufficient energy, by using his space distortion coils, to destroy the great projector mechanism. Instantly Arcot, now able to create the artificial space without the destruction of the coils by the struggling ray-feed coil, had thrown them to comparative safety.

Space writhed before they could so much as turn from the instruments. The Thessians had located their artificial space, and reached it with an attraction ray. They already had been withstanding the drain of the enormous fields of the giant planet and the giant sun; the attractive ray was an added strain. Arcot looked at his instruments, and with a grim smile set a single dial. The space about them became black again.

"Pulling our energy — merely let 'em pull. They're pulling on an ocean, not a lake this time. I don't think they'll drain those coils very quickly." He looked at his instruments. "Good for two and a half hours at this rate.

"Morey, you sure did your job then. I was helpless. The controls wouldn't answer, of course, with that titanic thing flopping its wings, so to speak. What are we going to do?"

Morey stood in the doorway, and from his pocket drew a cigarette, handed it to Arcot, another to each of the others who smoked, and lit them, and his own. "Smoke," he said, and puffed. "Smoke and think. From our last experience with a minor tragedy, it helps."

"But — this is no minor tragedy, they have burst open the wall of this invulnerable ship, destroyed one of those enormous coils, and can do it again," exclaimed Zezdon Afthen, exceedingly nervous, so nervous that the normal courage of the man was gone. His too-psychic breeding was against him as a warrior.

"Afthen," replied Stel Felso Theu calmly, "when our friends have smoked, and thought, the *Thought* will be repaired perfectly, and it will be made invulnerable to that weapon."

"I hope so, Stel Felso Theu," smiled Arcot. He was feeling better already. "But do you know what that weapon is, Morey?"

"Got some readings on it with the *Banderlog*'s instruments, and I think I do. Twin-ray is right," replied Morey.

"Hm-hm — so I think. It's a super-photon. What they do is to use a field somewhat similar to the field we use in making cosmium, except that in theirs, instead of the photons lying side by side, they slide into one another, compounding. They evidently get three photons to go into one. Now, as we know, that size photon doesn't exist for the excellent reason that it can't in this space. Space closes in about it. Therefore they have a projected field to accompany it that tends to open out space — and they are using that, not the attractive ray, on us now. The result is that for a distance not too great, the triple-ray exists in normal space — then goes into another. Now the question is how can we stop it? I have an idea — have you any?"

"Yes, but my idea can't exist in this space either," grinned Morey.

"I think it can. If it's what I think, remember it will have a terrific electric field."

"It's what you think, then. Come on." Arcot and Morey went to the calculating room, while Wade took over the ship. But one of the ray-feeds had been destroyed, and they had three more in action, as well as their most important weapon, artificial matter. Wade threw on the time field, and started the emergency lead burner working to recharge the coils that the Thessians were constantly draining. Being in their own peculiar space, they could not draw energy from the stars, and Arcot didn't want to return to normal space to discharge them, unless necessary.

"How's the air pressure in the rest of the ship?" asked Wade.

"Triple normal," replied Morey. "The Thessian atmosphere leaked in and sent it up terrifically, but when we went into our own space, at the halfway point, a lot leaked out. But the ship is full of water now. It was a bit difficult coming up from the *Banderlog*, and I didn't want to breathe the air I wasn't sure of. But let's work."

They worked. For eight hours of the time they were now in they continued to work. The supply of lead metal gave out before the end of the fourth hour, and the coils were nearing the end of their resistance. It would soon be necessary for Arcot to return to normal space. So they stopped, their calculations very nearly complete. Throwing all the remaining energy into the coils, they a little more than held the space about them, and moved away from Thett at a speed of about twice that of light. For an hour more Arcot worked, while the ship plowed on. Then they were ready.

As Arcot took over the controls, space reeled once more, and they were alone, far from Thett. The suns of this space were flashing and glowing about them, and the unlimited energy of a universe was at Arcot's command. But all the remaining atmosphere in the ship had either gone instantaneously in the vacuum, or solidified as the chill of expansion froze it.

To the amazement of the extra-terrestrians, Arcot's first move was to create a titanic plane of artificial matter, and neatly bisect the *Thought* at the middle! He had thrown all of the controls thus interrupted into neutral, and in the little more than half of the ship which contained the control cabin, was also the artificial matter control. It was busy now. With bewildering speed, with the speed of thought trained to construct, enormous masses of cosmium were appearing beside them in space as Arcot created them from pure energy. Cosmium, relux and some clear cosmium-like lux metal. Ordinary cosmium was reflective, and he wanted something with cosmium's strength, and the clearness of lux.

In seconds, under Arcot's flying thought manipulation, a great tube had been welded to the original hull, and the already gigantic ship lengthened by more than five hundred feet! Immediately great artificial matter tools gripped the broken nose-section, clamped it into place, and welded it with cosmium flowing under the inconceivable pressure till it was again a single great hull.

Then the Thessian fleet found them. The coils were charged now, and they could have escaped, but Arcot had to work. The Thessians were attacked with moleculars, cosmics, and a great twin-ray. Arcot could not use his magnet, for it had been among those things severed from the control. He had two ray feeds, and the artificial matter. There were nearly three thousand ships attacking him with a barrage of energy that was inconceivably great, but the cosmium walls merely turned it aside. It took Arcot less than ten seconds to wipe out that fleet of ships! He created a wall of artificial matter at twenty feet from the ship — and another at twenty thousand miles. It was thin, yet it was utterly impenetrable. He swept the two walls together, and forced them against each other until his instruments told him only free energy remained between them. Then he released the outer wall, and a terrific flood of energy swept out.

"I don't think we'll be attacked again," said Morey softly. They were not. Thett had only one other fleet, and had no intention of losing the powers of their generators at this time when they so badly needed them. The strange ship had retired for repairs — very well, they could attack again — and maybe —

Arcot was busy. In the great empty space that had been left, he installed a second collector coil as gigantic as the main artificial matter generator. Then he repaired the broken ray feed, and it, and the companion coil which, with it, had been in the severed nose section, were now in the same relative position to the new collector coil that they had had with relation to the artificial matter coil. Next Arcot built two more ray feeds. Now in the gigantic central power room there loomed two tremendous power collectors, and six smaller ray feed collectors.

His next work was to reconnect the severed connectors and controls. Then he began work on the really new apparatus. Nothing he had constructed so far was more than a duplicate of existing apparatus, and he had been able to do it almost instantly, from memory. Now he must vision something new to his experience, and something that was forced to exist in part in this space, and partly in another. He tried four times before the apparatus had been completed correctly, and the work occupied ten hours. But at last it was done. The *Thought* was ready now for the battle.

"Got it right at last?" asked Wade. "I hope so."

"It's right — tried it a little. I don't think you noticed it. I'm going down now to give them a nice little dose," said Arcot grimly. His ship was repaired — but they had caused him plenty of trouble.

"How long have we been out here, their time?" asked Wade.

"About an hour and a half." The *Thought* had been on the time field at all times save when the Thessian fleet attacked.

"I think, Earthman, that you are tired, and should rest, lest you make a tired thought and do great harm," suggested Zezdon Afthen.

"I want to finish it!" replied Arcot, sharply. He was tired.

In seconds the *Thought* was once more over that fortified station in the mountains — and the triple-ray reached out — and suddenly, about the ship, was a wall of absolute, utter blackness. The triple-ray touched it, and exploded into coruscating, blinding energy. It could not penetrate it. More energy lashed at the wall of blackness as the operators within the sphere-fort turned in the energy of all the generators under their control. The ground about the fort was a great lake of dazzling lava as far as the eye could see, for the triple-ray was releasing its energy, and the wall of black was releasing an equal, and opposing energy!

"Stopped!" cried Arcot happily. "Now here is where we give them something to think about. The magnet and the heat!"

He turned the two enormous forces simultaneously on the point where he knew the fort was, though it was invisible behind the wall of black that protected him. From his side, the energy of the spot where all the system of Thett was throwing its forces, was invisible.

Then he released them. Instantly there was a terrific gout of light on that wall of blackness. The ship trembled, and space turned gray about them. The black wall dissolved into grayness in one spot, as a flood of energy beyond comprehension exploded from it. The enormously strong cosmium wall dented as the pressure of the escaping radiation struck it, and turned X-ray hot under the minute percentage it absorbed. The triple-ray bent away, and faded to black as the cosmic force playing about it, actually twisted space beyond all power of its mechanism to overcome. Then, in the tiniest fraction of a second it was over, and again there was blackness and only the brilliant, blinding blue of the cosmium wall testified to its enormous temperature, cooling now far more slowly through green to red.

"Lord — you're right, Zezdon Afthen. I'm going to sleep," called Arcot. And the ship was suddenly far, far away from Thett. Morey took over, and Arcot slept. First Morey straightened the uninjured wall and ironed out the dents.

"What, Morey, is the wall of Blackness?" asked Stel Felso Theu.

"It's solid matter. A thing that you never saw before. That wall of matter is made of a double layer of protons lying one against the other. It absorbs absolutely every and all radiation, and because it is solid matter, not tiny sprinklings of matter in empty space, as is the matter of even the densest star, it stops the triple-ray. That matter is nothing but protons; there are no electrons there, and the positive electrical field is inconceivably great, but it is artificial matter, and that electrical field exerts its strain not in pulling and electrifying other bodies, but in holding space open, in keeping it from closing in about that concentrated matter, just as it does about a single proton, except that here the entire field energy is so absorbed.

"Arcot was tired, and forgot. He turned his magnet and his heat against it. The heat fought the solid matter with the same energy that created it, and with an energy that had resources as great. The magnet curved space about it, and about us. The result was the terrific energy release you saw, and the hole in the wall. All Thett couldn't make any impression on it. One of the rays blasted a hole in it," said Morey with a laugh. For he, too, loved this mighty thing, the almost living ideas of his friend's brain.

"But it is as bad as the space defense. It works both ways. We can't send through it but neither can they. Any thing we use that attacks them, attacks it, and so destroys it — and it fights."

"We're worse off than ever!" said Morey gloomily.

"My friend, you, too, are tired. Sleep, sleep soundly, sleep till I call — sleep!" And Morey slept under Zezdon Afthen's will, till Torlos carried him gently to his room. Then Afthen let the sleep relax to a natural one. Wade decided he might as well follow under his own power, for now he knew he was tired, and could not overcome Zezdon Afthen, who was not.

*****

On Thett, the fort was undestroyed, and now floating on its power units in a sea of blazing lava. Within, men were working quickly to install a second set of the new tubes in the molecular motion ray screen, and other men were transmitting the orders of the Sthanto who had come here as the place of actually greatest safety.

"Order all battleships to the nearest power-feed station, and command that all power available be transmitted to the station attacked. I believe it will be this one. There is no limit on the power transmission lines, and we need all possible power," he commanded his son, now in charge of all land and spatial forces.

"And Ranstud, what happened to that molecular ray screen?"

"I do not know. I cannot understand such power.

"But what most worries me is his wall of darkness," said Ranstud seriously.

"But he was forced to retire for all his wall of darkness, as you saw.

"He can maintain it but a short time, and it was full of holes when he fled."

"Old Sthanto is much too confident, I believe," said an assistant working at one of the great boards in the enemy's fort, to one of his friends. "And I think he has lost his science-knowledge. Any power-man could tell what happened. They tried to use their own big rays against us, and their screen stopped them from going out, just as it stopped ours on the way in. Ours had been working at it for seconds, and hadn't bothered them. Then for a bare instant their ray touched it — and they retired. That shield of blackness is absolutely new."

"They have many men on that ship of theirs," replied his friend, helping to lift the three hundred ton load of a vacuum tube into place, "for it is evident that they built new apparatus, and it is evident their ship was increased in size to contain it. Also the nose was repaired. They probably worked under a time field, for they accomplished an impossible amount of work in the period they were gone."

Ranstud had come up behind them, and overheard the later part of this conversation. "And what," he asked suddenly, "did your meters tell you when our ray opened his ship?"

"Councilor of Science-wisdom, they told us that our power diminished, and our generators gave off but little power when his power was exceedingly little, we still had much."

"Have you heard the myth of the source of his power, in the story that he gets it from all the stars of the Island?"

"We have, Great Councilor. And I for one believe it, for he sucked the power from our generators. So might he suck the power from the inconceivably greater generators of the Suns. I believe that we should treat with them, for if they be like the peace-loving fools of Venone, we might win a respite in which to learn their secret."

Ranstud walked away slowly. He agreed, in his heart, but he loved life too well to tell the Sthanto what to do, and he had no intention of sacrificing himself for the possible good of the race.

So they prepared for another attack of the *Thought*, and waited.

CHAPTER XXVI

MAN, CREATOR AND DESTROYER

"What we must find," said Arcot, between contented puffs, for he had slept well, and his breakfast had been good, "is some weapon which will attack them, but won't attack us. The question is, what is it? And I think, I think — I know." His eyes were dreamy, his thoughts so cryptically abbreviated that not even Morey could follow them.

"Fine — what is it?" asked Morey after vainly striving to deduce some sense from the formulas that were chasing through Arcot's thoughts. Here and there he recognized them: Einstein's energy formula, Planck's quantum formulas, Nitsu Thansi's electron interference formulas, Stebkowfski's proton interference, Williamson's electric field, and his own formulas appeared, and others so abbreviated he could not recognize them.

"Do you remember what Dad said about the way the Thessians made the giant forts out in space — hauled matter from the moon and transformed it to lux and relux. Remember, I said then I thought it might be a ray — but found it wasn't what I thought? I want to to use the ray I was thinking of. The only question in my mind is — what is going to happen to us when I use it?"

"What's the ray?"

"Why is it, Morey, that an electron falls through the different quantum energy levels, falls successively lower and lower till it reaches its 'lowest energy level,' and can radiate no more. Why can't it fill another step, and reach the proton? Why has it no more quanta to release? We know that electrons tend to fall always to lower energy level orbits. Why do they stop?"

"And," said Morey, his own eyes dreamily bright now, "what would happen if it did? If it fell all the way?"

"I cannot follow your thoughts, Earthmen, beyond a glimpse of an explosion. And it seems it is Thett that is exploding, and that Thett is exploding itself. Can you explain?" asked Stel Felso Theu.

"Perhaps — you know that electrons in their planetary orbits, so called, tend to fall away to orbits of lower energy, till they reach the lowest energy orbit, and remain fixed till more energy comes and is absorbed, driving them out again. Now we want to know why they don't fall lower, fall all the way? As a matter of fact, thanks to some work I did last year with disintegrating lead, we do know. And thanks to the absolute stability of artificial matter, we can handle such a condition.

"The thing we are interested in is this: Artificial matter has no tendency to radiate, its electrons have no tendency to fall into the proton, for the matter is created, and remains as it was created. But natural matter does have a tendency to let the electron fall into the proton. A force, the 'lowest energy wall,' over which no electron can jump, caused by the enormous space distorting of the proton's mass and electrical attraction, prevents it. What we want to do is to remove that force, iron it out. Requires inconceivable power to do so in a mass the size of Thett-but then — !

"And here's what will happen: Our wall of protonic material won't be affected by it in the least, because it has no tendency to collapse, as has normal matter, but Thett, beyond the wall, *has* hat tendency, and the ray will release the energy of every planetary electron on Thett, and every planetary electron will take with it the energy of one proton. And it will take about one one-hundred-millionth of a second. Thett will disappear in one instantaneous flash of radiation, radiation in the high cosmics!

"Here's the trouble: Thett represents a mass as great as our sun. And our sun can throw off energy at the present rate of one sol for a period of some ten million million years, three and a half million tons of matter a second for ten million years. If all of that went up in *one one-hundred-millionth of a second*, how many sols?" asked Morey.

"Too many, is all I can say. Even this ship couldn't maintain its walls of energy against that!" declared Stel Felso Theu, awed by the thought.

"But that same power would be backing this ship, and helping it to support its wall. We would operate from — half a million miles."

"We will. If we are destroyed — so is Thett, and all the worlds of Thett. Let that flood of energy get loose, and everything within a dozen light years will be destroyed. We will have to warn the Venonians, that their people on nearby worlds may escape in the time before the energy reaches them," said Arcot slowly.

The *Thought* started toward one of the nearer suns, and as it went, Arcot and Morey were busy with the calculators. They finished their work, and started back from that world, having given their message of warning, with the artificial matter constructors. When they reached Thett, less than a quarter of an hour of Thessian time had passed. But, before they reached Thett, Arcot's viewplates were blinded for an instant as a terrific flood of energy struck the artificial matter protectors, and caused them to flame into defense. Thett's satellite was sending its message of instantaneous destruction. That terrific ray had reached it, touched it, and left it a shattered, glowing ball of hydrogen.

"There won't be even that left when we get through with Thett!" said Arcot grimly. The apparatus was finished, and once more they were over the now fiery-red lava sea that had been mountains. The fort was still in action. Arcot had cut a sheet of sheer energy now, and as the triple-ray struck it, he knew what would happen. It did. The triple-ray shunted off at an angle of forty-five degrees in the energy field, and spread instantly to a diffused beam of blackness. Arcot's molecular reached out. The lava was instantly black, and mountains of ice were forming over the struggling defenses of the fort. The molecular screen was working.

"I'd like to know how they make tubes that'll stand that, Morey," said Arcot, pointing to an instrument that read .01 millisols. "They have tubes now, that would have wiped us out in minutes, seconds before this."

The triple-ray snapped off. They were realigning it to hit the ship now, correcting for the shield. Arcot threw out his protonic shield, and retreated to half a million miles, as he had said.

"Here goes." But before even his thoughts could send Theft to radiation, the entire side of the planet blazed suddenly incandescent. Thett was learning what had happened when their ray had wounded the *Thought*.

And then, in the barest instant of time, there was no Thett. There was an instant of intolerable radiation, then momentary blackness, and then the stars were shining where Thett had been. Thett was utterly gone.

But Arcot did not see this. About him there was a tremendous roar, titanic generator-converters that had not so much as hummed under the impact of Thett's greatest weapons, whined and shuddered now. The two enormous generators, the blackness of the protonic shield, and the great artificial matter generator, throwing an inner shield impervious to the cosmics Thett gave off as it vanished, both were whining. And the six smaller machines, which Arcot had succeeded in interconnecting with the protonic generator, were whining too. Space was weirdly distorted, glowing gray about them, the great generators struggling to maintain the various walls of protecting power against the surge of energy as Thett, a world of matter, disintegrated.

But the Very energy that fought to destroy those walls was

absorbed in defending it, and by that much the attacking energy was lessened. Still, it seemed hours, days that the battle of forces continued.

Then it was over, and the skies were clear once more as Arcot lowered the protonic screen silently. The white sky of Thett was gone, and only the black starriness of space remained.

"*It's gone!*" gasped Torlos. He had been expecting it — still, the disappearance of a world —

"We will have to do no more. No ships had time to escape, and the risk we run is too great," said Morey slowly. "The escaping energy from that world will destroy the others of this system as completely, and it will probably cause the sun itself to blow up — perhaps to form new planets, and so the process repeats itself. But Venone knows better now, and their criminals will not populate more worlds.

"And we can go — home. To our little dust specks."

"But they're wonderfully welcome dust specks, and utterly important to us, Earthman," reminded Zezdon Afthen.

"Let us go then," said Arcot.

*****

It was dusk, and the rose tints of the recently-set sun still hung on the clouds that floated like white bits of cotton in the darkening blue sky. The dark waters of the little lake, and the shadowy tree-clad hills seemed very beautiful. And there was a little group of buildings down there, and a broad cleared field. On the field rested a shining, slim shape, seventy-five feet long, ten feet in diameter.

But all, the lake, the mountains even, were dwarfed by the silent, glistening ruby of a gigantic machine that settled very, very slowly, and very, very gently downward. It touched the rippled surface of the lake with scarcely a splash, then hung, a quarter submerged in that lake.

Lights were showing in the few windows the huge bulk had, and lights showed now in the buildings on the shore. Through an open door light was streaming, casting silhouettes of two men. And now a tiny door opened in the enormous bulk that occupied the lake, and from it came five figures, that floated up, and away, and toward the cottage.

"Hello, Son. You have been gone long," said Arcot, senior, gravely, as his son landed lightly before him.

"I thought so. Earth has moved in her orbit. More than six months?"

His father smiled a bit wryly. "Yes. Two years and three

months. You got caught in another time field and thrown the other way this time?"

"Time and force. Do you know the story yet?"

"Part of it — Venone sent a ship to us within a month of the time you left, and said that all Thett's system had disappeared save for one tremendous gas cloud — mostly hydrogen. Their ships were met by such a blast of cosmic rays as they came toward Thett that the radiation pressure made it almost impossible to advance. There were two distinct waves. One was rather slighter, and was more in the gamma range, so they suspected that two bodies had been directly destroyed; one small one, and one large one were reduced completely to cosmics. Your warning to Sentfenn was taken seriously, and they have vacated all planets near. It was the force field created when you destroyed Thett that threw you forward? Where are the others?"

"Zezdon Afthen and Zezdon Inthel we took home, and dropped in their power suits, without landing. Stel Felso Theu as well. We will visit them later."

"Have you eaten? Then let us eat, and after supper we'll tell you what little there is to tell."

"But Arcot," said Morey slowly, "I understand that Dad will be here soon, so let us wait. And I have something of which I have not spoken to you as yet. Worked it out and made it on the back trip. Installed in the *Thought* with the *Banderlog*'s controls. It is — well, will you look? — Fuller! Come and see the new toy you designers are going to have to work on!"

They had all been depressed by the thought of their long absence, by the scenes of destruction they had witnessed so recently. They were beginning to feel better.

"Watch." Morey's thoughts concentrated. The *Thought* outside had been left on locked controls, but the apparatus Morey had installed responded to his thoughts from this distance.

Before them in the room appeared a cube that was obviously copper. It stayed there but a moment, beaming brightly, then there was a snapping of energies about them — and it dropped to the floor and rang with the impact!

"It was not created from the air," said Morey simply.

"And now," said Arcot, looking at it, "Man can do what never before was possible. From the nothingness of Space he can make anything.

"Man alone in this space is Creator and Destroyer.

"It is a high place.

"May he henceforth live up to it."

And he looked out toward the mighty starlit hull that had destroyed a solar system — and could create another.

THE END

CPSIA information can be obtained
at www.ICGtesting.com
Printed in the USA
LVOW11s1814180917
549136LV00001B/74/P